SIN CITY
LOVE FORBIDDEN

SIN CITY
LOVE FORBIDDEN

JENNIFER MARIE THIGPEN

CITIOFBOOKS, INC.
3736 Eubank NE Suite A1
Albuquerque, NM 87111-3579
www.citiofbooks.com

Hotline: 1 (877) 389-2759
Fax: 1 (505) 930-7244

Ordering Information:
Quantity sales. Special discounts are available on quantity purchases by corporations, associations, and others. For details, contact the publisher at the address above.

Printed in the United States of America.

ISBN-13: Paperback   979-8-89391-831-1
          eBook   979-8-89391-832-8

Library of Congress Control Number: 2025915266

TABLE OF CONTENTS

Dedication

This book is dedicated to my husband, James Thigpen. Without him, I would not be here today. He came back into my life at a time when I needed him the most. We were told, a long time ago, to stay away from each other, but we did not listen. That was the best decision I have ever made. I Love You, James. I hope you are proud of me for finally conquering my fear of being rejected and following my heart. It had been far too long.

HISTORICAL INFORMATION
PHENIX CITY'S CORRUPT PAST

Phenix City, Alabama had not earned the name "Wickedest City in the USA" and later known as the original "Sin City," by total accident. In the beginning she was known as the home of the Muscogee Indians, who were the first victims of European crimes. Though these people had lived by their own laws and customs for bad behavior and rule breaking for generations. It still led to a clash as to what authorities called "savage." European's moving onto their lands led to raids, retaliations, and ruthless executions of settlers and natives alike for those who had moved into the Alabama frontier. This brutal way of life finally crumbled the Indigenous empire and caused damage to this part of Alabama for more than a century.

By 1900, the small village of Girard, which was located on the banks of the Chattahoochee River, was known as a hideout for outlaws and as a place of vice. Immigrants brought with them the art of brewing and distilling spirits, which had earned the village the nickname, "Sodom." Many of the first settlers made a living from the making of these spirits and would do just about anything to protect their way of life.

By the 1950's, Phenix City was seen as another border town like Tijuana, Mexico. A town that offered soldiers, at Fort Benning, Georgia, every type of pleasure the soldiers could imagine, and these soldier, who were away from home for the first time, could imagine plenty. Phenix City's neighbors would not get involved in trying to help residents drive the criminal element out of the small city. Other cities that wanted to keep their reputation intact stayed away from the small southern town. Being associated with Phenix City might lead to their being seen in the world's eyes as a place of moral turpitude, and their neighbors could not afford the stigma. Most towns of the time believed future generations would see them as being like Phenix City and believe them too to be guilty of the same kind of crimes as their neighbor if only by association.

Columbus, Georgia could not give soldiers anything like Phenix City had for the young and old males alike of surrounding communities. Even comparing and calling Phenix City another Tijuana might be an insult to Mexico because this small town was worse in every way than anything Tijuana had to offer.

From World War II to the mid fifty's, the mob ran Phenix City. Mob bosses would send what they called mobile units to meet the extra demands. Soldiers could find girls handing out their favors under tarps from the back of pickup trucks. There were casinos behind every door downtown. Mafia bosses arranged for playing cards to be marked by experts, who lived in the town, in a warehouse located nearby. They also loaded dice for use at the town's casinos. "B-girls hired to get soldiers drunk enough that they lost their boots at the roulette wheel. When soldiers woke the next morning, they were horrified to find their boots had been sold to the local Pawn shops or he had been rolled on his way to Ma Beachies Swing Time Club just up the street. Everyone considered Ma Beachies to be the local grandmother figure. Someone who visited Mas regularly once said, "Ma keeps a matching pair of pistols under the counter for customers who got out of hand."

The city's government was known throughout the south as the mob's puppets. Those found to be in the mob's pocket were the police chief, sheriff, judges, and jurors. In those days everyone belonged to the mob. It was a well-known fact if someone complained about what was going on in Phenix City law enforcement would throw them in jail. These ruthless representatives of the law had a reputation of making up charges and bringing those they accused of being troublemakers in on drunk and disorderly charges. These charges would be used to keep anyone from making trouble for the businesses owned by the Mafia downtown. Many of these men were fitted with a pair of concrete over shoes and thrown into the Chattahoochee River where they could take a permanent swim with the fishes.

State Officials said Phenix City had been notorious dating back to the nineteenth century, when the city had been known as Girard. In those years, everyone knew the business owners for bootlegging, gambling, and one or two houses of ill repute. Now after World War II it was a multi-million-dollar business too big to fail. They were making enough money to bribe everyone in the State's government to keep those who might want to try closing them down.

*****

Occasionally somebody at Fort Benning would threaten to close Phenix City to soldiers permanently. Unlucky soldiers who did not have enough money to pay their debts would wind up dead. It was the Secretary of the Army who first called Phenix City the Wickedest City in the USA. In the 1940's when George S. Patton was the Commander at Fort Benning, he threatened to flatten Phenix City with one of his tanks.

Nothing ever came of any of these threats, when officials looked at the facts, higher-ups always reached the same conclusion. Soldiers needed somewhere to have fun. They were serving their country. All soldiers knew was any day military officials could send them to a foreign land to fight and never come home. Attitudes towards Phenix City became one of laissez-faire, it is serving the good of the service men, so they would let them do as they pleased in their town. Phenix City's criminal activities became normal. An extensive line of governors and state Attorney General would look the other way because of campaign promises, backdoor bribes or because other issues in the state were more important. No one at the state level was calling for the city's clean up. The only ones calling for someone to clean the city up was a growing number of citizens from Phenix City. Included in those that wanted the city cleaned up was Hugh Bentley, he was the man who started the Russell Betterment Association. He opened himself up to threats, some were against his life for having the gumption to stand up against these Mafia bosses. One day someone blew his house up as a warning to him, that it would be best if he kept his mouth shut. Everyone in town knew, however, it was because of his affiliation with the Russell Betterment Association.

*****

Bama and Corral Clubs were the clubs in town where patrons could find big-time gambling. These clubs advertised and attracted suckers from all over the south. Reservations were often necessary to get into one of these clubs. A person could find every type of gambling known to man while they were in Phenix City. Games available during a nightly visit included: lottery, slots, blackjack, parlays on football, baseball, and basketball. Clubs were known to maintain a large stock of fireworks. Clipjoint specialists of the time were Stewart McCollister, J. D. Abney, Clyde Yarbrough, and J. D. (Frog) Jones. These club owners were known to provide services to men with a highly inflated price.

Golden Rule café, located at 1500 3rd Avenue was another of these Clubs. Today you will find the Courtyard by Marriott and Troy University located on this block. Inside the Golden Rule there were four slot machines, three horse racing machines, a pinball machine, and a large poker table which was located upstairs. They once refused to let the Army investigator enter the building. The Golden rule was owned and operated by France Knighton poet laureate of the gambling world. France would dress in the most outlandish clothes. His suits consisted of loud-colored cap, red-checkered shirt, and pink trousers. France spent his spare time writing poems about the stealing of elections, the Russell Betterment Association, and on most occasions the gamblers themselves.

One-night after the Governor had declared Martial Rule, France Knighton asked Major General Walter J. Hanna for his license back. General Hanna was under orders to take all the licenses from the businesses in Phenix City. Hanna then made France a counterproposal, "if he would swear there was no gambling going on inside his establishment, he would give him back his license." A statement which Hanna knew was a lie and would cause Knighton to perjure himself. Instead, Knighton collected his cap and walked to the police station instead. A department hours before Alabama National Guard had taken control of the duties of both the Chief of Police and his officers.

The Bluebonnet was another of these places of ill repute. It was a place where you could find gambling, prostitution, and tattooing. Anything a young man or older gentleman wanted he could find at the Bluebonnet. All done to the pleasure of all who visited while the men waited. Your host for the evening, at the Bluebonnet, would have been Frank Gullatt.

Times in this book are based on true events in a small southern town called Phenix City. Phenix City is on the Alabama, Georgia line in the central part of the state. In 1954, Albert Patterson was murdered as he got into his car which was parked beside his law office. Historical events are true, with a little poetic license taken to make the book more enjoyable. The love affair between the soldier and the prostitute is fictional. It is something good that could have come out of such an ugly time in Phenix City, Alabama's past.

"It was just too lucrative to quit because that meant double pay – the soldier paid for the girl and the girl paid for protection – and the money kept pyramiding and with it, power." Margaret Ann Barnes, The Tragedy and the Triumph of Phenix City, Alabama

EIGHTEEN YEARS AFTER THE DEATH OF ALBERT PATTERSON
MARK MITCHELL – THE STORY BEGINS

As the years rolled slowly by, Brian Wilchar's horrible death behind Ma Beachies Swing Time Club had been the making for Mark Mitchell some of the most beautiful years of his life. While US Marshals sat telling Mark the grotesque way his best friend, Brian Wilchair, had spent his last few minutes on earth. Mark stood still, listening to every detail the man told him. Details which were so horrifying they made his entire body shake. In the time, Mark stood there listening to the new, he made a promise to himself. Brian's child would grow up happy and somehow have the life he knew Brian would have given his son if he had been allowed to live.

Brian came from a family who owned half of Pine Mountain Valley, but when they found out their son was going to be a father, they turned their backs on their first-born grandchild. Mark knew in his heart, if it had been him the National Guard had found that morning behind Ma's, Brian would have taken care of his child, and the mother in a fashion that would make his friend proud; to have called him friend.

Years after his birth Brian Wilchair Mitchell would invite friends over to his home in the hopes, he could get his father to tell, anyone who would listen, the story of how he came into this world. Mark and Lacey made no differences between Brian and their other children. In his parents' eyes, if Brian was happy, just knowing his parents loved him and wanted what was best for him, meant the world to them. They would do anything for the boy to make sure he was happy. If telling his friends, the story over and over made him take a special kind of pride in himself, Mark would tell anyone who would sit and listen to the story of his friend's horrible death and the birth of his son. It was the least he could do for his friend, and the son Brian Wilchar never got the chance to know or have the pleasure of seeing grow up. All because somebody wanted everyone to keep their distance from the property of the owners of the brothels in the area.

"Daddy, will you tell me and my friends the story of my birth? I want them to hear this special story of how my parents met each other and in the brief time they had together fell in love." Brian requested this story be told by the man who had raised him every chance he got. He loved the story and wanted everyone to know the circumstances surrounding his birth.

Mark Mitchell was happiest when he was given the chance to tell others the special story. He had known Brian's father since the two men were in the 10th grade back in Pine Mountain, Georgia. Mark had grown up down the road from the Wilchar horse farm and found a different kind of happiness in the pastures of green grass while he sat watching the horses roam the property.

Mark could think of nothing he enjoyed more than spending time with his son. A youngster who made Mark feel at peace with himself and close to the friend he had lost years before. Brian made him see himself in a way nothing or no one else could.

"Sure, Brian, I will, it does my heart good to know you want to hear stories about your father," Brian may have been someone else's child biologically, but Mark could not have been prouder of the young man he was becoming. Mark had taken on the responsibility of Brian the day he and his mom found out she was pregnant. Men employed by Ma Beachies murdered his father several hours before his mother got the news, she was going to have a baby. She did not get the chance to tell anybody about her pregnancy. That morning the agent drove up in her driveway and broke the news to her and Mark of Brian's gruesome death. Lacey could not bring herself to tell anyone her news. She was heartbroken and scared all at once. Lacey was unsure what was going to happen to her, but she knew, she had to protect her unborn child from the powers that be in Phenix City.

****

In Phenix City in the early 1950's it was an age of violence; law-abiding citizens knew they were to stay home at night or take the chance of being shot by a stray bullet or worse found the next morning floating in the River. No one wanted to take their lives in their own hands by going into town after dark. Crime in downtown had taken hold and anyone who got in the way of their activities would be sure to find a sudden end. You could get into all the trouble you could think of in Phenix City in those days gambling, girls, and alcohol. It involved everyone, whether you made it to the banks of the Chattahoochee River on foot or by car. When you arrived in the city at the river's edge, you could find any kind of pleasure you were of a mind to find. Nothing was too outlandish if you could conceive of it, you could find your heart's desire in Phenix City. For those who were in charge in those days knew what men wanted and had found a lucrative way to give it to all who were looking for a good time from their kind of services.

Fort Benning, the Army base built to the south of Columbus, Georgia was the main source of patrons for these seedy business owners. Officials on-base issued orders with every new class of men entering basic training. These orders required soldiers to stay out of Phenix City. Everyone knew with the proximity of the city to the base nobody really expected the men to give up the chance to have a good time. Women and the prospect of cash were a compelling temptation. The very thought of women brought the men from the base to the city every weekend. Soldiers made their way to "Sin City" with or without the consent of those in charge. When the Commanding Officer at Fort Benning suggested his soldiers stay away from the modest town after two of their own had gotten themselves rolled and other unmentionable things done to them one hot, steamy Friday night. Soldiers would come to town for a little fun, and on many Friday nights they found more than they bargained for. Every Friday and Saturday night, soldiers would take their chances in Sin City. Soldiers found the draw of the city was too much for the men to pass up. Even the prospect of contracting a sexually transmitted disease did not stop the steady stream of soldiers lusting for the time of their lives.

Base officials had told recruits to stay out of Phenix City it was forbidden to them, but they would come across the bridge from Columbus for the girls and the gambling. Business owners were using the pleasures available in the town to tempt soldiers to come to their places of business to lose their money. They had warned men from Fort Benning they were putting themselves in danger just going across the bridge. Bouncers at the clubs along the bridge rolled men who came into the city. If they did not lose their lives that night, it was a fact everyone would lose their paychecks before they were allowed to leave the next morning. Unfortunately, those who did not leave were beaten or worse. Authorities in the City of Columbus would find unsuspecting strangers to the city in the river where the bouncers had dumped the twisted, beaten bodies when the girls or the managers of the Clubs finished stealing what they could from them.

Phenix City, Alabama in 1954 was in turmoil and was proving to be a community in trouble. Since Phenix City favored their hometown feel so much, citizens assumed they could manage whatever came their way. People in the small-town thought nothing like what the residents in neighboring towns were describing could happen where they called home.

Crime ran rampant in Phenix City in the early 1950s. Law enforcement, District Attorney's Office and City Hall were all controlled by the local crime bosses. If citizens were to luck up and be given protection from corruption, they had to be part of the system which ran Phenix City, or a business that was being shook down and paying the crime bosses to keep them safe. Law Enforcement was not there to protect the honest man from the forces that had taken control in this small town. They were there to protect the Mafia bosses who ran the southern town during the time of prohibition, and for a little while thereafter. After prohibition, the mafia found no reason to leave. They were making money, and that was all they cared about. They could bring in people from other parts of the country. In club's people could buy their way into the games and come to town to play in these high paying games on any given Friday night.

My story started here:

MARK ALEXANDER MITCHELL

A bundle of joy that was welcomed into this world on June 12, 1933, in Concord, Georgia. Concord, to this day, has no red lights; cars are a rare sight in town. Quiet, peaceful town in the county of Pike just up the road from Thomaston, Georgia. When people visualize Concord, they would give the surrounding countryside and horse farms a shout out as a town suitable for small families. Where they could still live the old ways. Residents in Concord still rode their horses into Zebulon to get their groceries. Life in the small country town was slower and more family friendly than the rest of the State.

Mark was born the sixth child of his parents growing family. Everyone considered six kids in the early thirty's a small family. Most people of the day had thirteen or more children; especially boys, parents needed them to help in the fields. Whenever he got the chance, his family would find him playing cops and robbers. His mom once found Mark pretending to be a US Marshal. Everyone in Concord had fond memories of him pretending to catch the bad guys outside his own or his town. Mark lived to catch the bad guys and save those who the criminal elements in town had taken advantage. When he pretended to arrest the crooks in the county, it provided him with a sense of calmness in his heart. From an early age, he had a knack for figuring out who the person was that had committed the worst of the worst crimes around town.

Mark's parents were Charles Alexander Mitchell and Gretchen Virginia Howell. Charles and Ginny were married August 8, 1922, in Zebulon, Georgia at the County Courthouse. A year after the wedding, Ginny found out she was pregnant with their first child. His parents were blessed with six children before Mark. Charles and Ginny would have five children, including Mark live to adulthood. They were well on their way to getting everything they ever wanted. Including Mark, his parents were blessed with two boys and four girls. One of his older sisters died within her first six days of life from Typhoid Fever. His parents did not think to give the newborn a name, which in those days was a common way of doing things. Everyone who knew them always called her, baby girl and that is the way her grave is marked in the Hebron Cemetery there in Concord. After her death, Marks' parents showered their remaining children with all they could manage to buy them with their mediocre salary as sharecroppers. There was always food on the dinner table and clothes on their backs, and to the Mitchell's they felt as though they had been blessed with an over-abundance. Their kids never did want for anything, and to any parent that is all they could ask for.

As a kid, spending his younger years in a town known to residents for its beautiful farms made it tough for Mark to make friends near his home. After school during the week, Mark had to help his dad in the cotton fields that belonged to James Pendleton Mangham. James' family came to Pike County in the early 1800s when Pike County opened to settlers. The Mangham family was related to the founding families and was one of the better known.

When the Mitchell 's settled in Concord, Mark's family worked the land for other more well to do landowners. They would pick cotton for the Mangham's, and in return they would pay his dad a wage. Part of his income included a place for the family to live. People were known to travel around the county as the crops ripened and were ready for harvest. Mark's family did not move with the crops. They remained in the area and continued this type of work until around 1949 when Charles and Gretchen died.

Details that were included in the county paper of the afternoon Charles and Gretchen lost their lives while picking the years cotton crop were unsettling for the residents. A mare had gotten loose, and field hands saw it as it began to run through the field. Charles decided he was going to try to stop the mare by snagging the rope dragging behind her. When he caught the rope, the mare was too strong for him and drug him about one hundred yards before field hands could get her to stop.

When Mr. Mangham got to Charles and the mare, he was already bleeding from his mouth. As he lay there on the ground James Mangham sent one of the field hands to the house to call the sheriff. By the time the sheriff got to the orchard, it was too late. Charles had already succumbed to his injuries. As the Sheriff and his men walked the field, they found Gretchen Mitchell laying in the field where she had been standing when her husband grabbed for the rope.

Unaware of the injuries to Gretchen who had been standing beside her husband when he reached down for the rope. No one thought to go back and check on her. Gretchen had seen the large rocks all around where she was standing, but it all happened so fast there was no way she could avoid hitting her head on one of them. Someone had placed a few rocks in that part of the cotton field for the field workers to take their breaks on. When the mare raced by Charles, and as he caught the rope his leg bumped hers knocking Gretchen down. When she fell, she struck her head on the corner of one of the larger rocks and died before anyone realized she had been accidently hurt that afternoon.

With the death of both of his parents, he and his other siblings would need someone to take care of them. Families in town came to make the kids part of their households for a few weeks after that horrible day, but none of their friends and neighbors wanted to take in all the younger children together. It was a nightmare for a while, with younger children begging the Sheriff to find them a place where they could stay together, As the oldest, Emmaline had been raised with the knowledge that if something ever happened to her parents, it would be her responsibility to take care of the arrangements for the funeral and her younger brothers and sisters. While Emmaline made the arrangements for the burial and made certain she was able to provide the younger kids a roof over their heads and clothes on their backs, she was also looking for another place of employment. Emmaline knew she was going to need a larger house if her siblings were going to live with her, but she was determined to keep everyone together as her parents had always told her they wanted.

****

Emmaline was born on July 20, 1923, in the small town of Molena, Georgia. She had been groomed by her parents to take care of the family if something happened to them, and Emmaline had learned her lessons well.

Before their parent's funeral, she went to Pine Mountain to look for a job as a teacher. As luck would have it, she found a position at the local elementary school. After the funeral, Emmaline packed her siblings up in her old car, packed what belongings they could carry, and alone, she moved her entire family to Pine Mountain, Georgia.

****

Alexander Benjamin Mitchell, Alex, as he liked to be called, was born May 21, 1925. He had always been the outcast of the family. Everyone expected him to leave town when he came of age. Alex never showed up at school on a regular basis and was

15

known by most of the town and his parents to be waiting for his sixteenth birthday so he could join the Army. He did not disappoint any of them, he enlisted in the Army the day he turned sixteen. He had served one tour of duty when he decided he did not want to serve his Country any longer. It was either take an honorable discharge or take the chance of the Army learning he had been involved in some of the most unscrupulous behavior in most of the places he had been stationed. It was only a matter of time before everyone knew it had been him that had beaten a few of the other soldiers to death over girls and money.

He did not return to Concord after his discharge, Alex moved to a small town called Phenix City. Once in the Alabama town he found work with Ma Beachies. He was given the position as her head bodyguard, and he alone made certain everyone got their assignments every day, rain, or shine. There was no move made at Ma's that Alex did not know about.

Alex being a couple of years younger than his sister he did not want to get in her way. He found out about his parent's death from a friend who had come to Ma's to gamble the night before. Alex was heartbroken when he was told what had happened to his parents. Nothing or no one could keep him from their funeral. He had no intentions of making anyone mad, so he stood under an oak tree to observe and listen to the service. None of his siblings would know he had been there. None of the younger children remembered him or when he left. Alex wanted to offer Emmaline his help by offering to take some of the younger children with him, but he knew she would never allow him to do anything to help her. He knew Emmaline was going to have her hands full with the children and her job. His problem was he did not have any idea how to approach her about their sharing the responsibility of their siblings. So, after the funeral he gave up on the notion and left town without ever telling anyone he was there, but someone did see him. Emmaline had noticed him standing under the tree and had every intention of talking to her brother, but by the time she got to where he had been standing, he had disappeared.

Neither Alex nor Emmaline ever knew it but someone else had seen Alex that day and recognized him. Mark, even though he was the youngest, did recognize his older brother and had wondered why he was not with him and the rest of the family during the funeral. Mark never said anything to Emmaline about seeing Alex that day, but the memory of his older brother, standing under that oak tree, stayed with him the rest of his life.

****

Amanda Elaine Mitchell was also born in Zebulon, Georgia. She came into the world on April 8, 1927. After Mandy graduated from high school, she took two years off to travel and work before beginning her college days at the University of Alabama in Tuscaloosa. She had since her childhood wanted to be a schoolteacher and now; she was making her dream come true.

Before her parents' death, she had been in Tuscaloosa for about six months . She did not come home often to see any of her family. Something had happened between Mandy and her parents before she left on her trip and beginning work. She made a point of staying away from the family home. None of her siblings knew how to find her, or so they all thought, giving them no way to send her the news of her of her parent's death or funeral. With none of the kids knowing how to reach her, it was hoped, someday, she would come home.

Nobody ever asked Mark Mitchell anything. They thought he was too young to remember his siblings, but he was not. He knew where his older siblings were and had been writing to both of them since they left home. Mark would receive letters and packages from both his siblings on occasion, but he hid them where nobody would ever find them. Mark was as good at hiding things as he was finding out what was going on in the nearby community. Without Emmaline's knowledge Mark had sent a letter to his sister telling her of the death of her parents a couple days before the funeral.

Emmaline knew in her heart, Mandy was going to be upset when she found out about her parents, but since she had no way of contacting her, Emmaline would have to deal with her feelings later. When the day came that Mandy did find out about her parents,' Emmaline knew it would be a devastating blow to her and hit her sister hard, but Emmaline would face that problem when she had to. For now, she was not going to worry about it, she had to care for her other siblings as best she could.

****

Elizabeth Susan Mitchell was born December 26, 1929, in Thomaston, Georgia. Her mom and the rest of the family had gone to Thomaston to visit one of her aunts. While they were there enjoying dinner during their annual Christmas visit, her water broke, and labor began. Her aunt called the Doctor to her home, and he delivered the baby after 24 hours of hard labor. Gretchen stayed at her aunts for another couple of days before Charles came back to Thomaston to fetch his wife and his new daughter.

As Liz grew up, she became a beautiful young lady. Her father doted on her. She was always with him and would whenever she got the chance work in the fields with him when school was out for spring break or the summer. Liz decided early she was not going to college she preferred to get married and have a family of her own.

While still in high school, she met the captain of the football team. Over the years they became good friends and spent as much of their time together as they were allowed. When they were juniors and seniors in school, they attended the prom together. Neither of them ever thought about dating anyone else. To them, there was no one else. Liz accepted a proposal of marriage from

Heath Barrett, and they planned to be married two weeks after graduation.

At the time of her parent's death, Liz had already given her parents two grandchildren who they were providing for what they could. Liz was planning to have more when word of her parent's death reached her. Their death hit her hard and no one would know until the day of their funeral if she was going to be able to attend with the rest of the family. Liz was so overcome with grief she was unable to make their funeral. She had to settle for her husband and children going in her place.

****

Sarah Ann Mitchell was the baby girl. Her parents allowed her to get away with all sorts of things they would never have thought of letting the other children get away with. Sarah was always a handful. Her parent's death hit her hard, and to forget what had happened to them, she started hanging around with the bad boys in the community. After the funeral it got so bad that Sarah took pleasure in getting into trouble more and more. Everyone in town knew that sooner or later her newfound friends would get Sarah into something no one could get her out of.

Emmaline had no idea what she was going to do with her baby sister. She was anxious as to what the Sheriff might come to her door next to tell her. Two years after her parent's death the day Emmaline had dreaded for more years than she wanted to admit, finally happened. The Sheriff drove up in the front yard and told her,

"Sarah is in jail. I arrested her last night after she and some of her friends broke into the General Store."

"Is there anything we can work out to get her out this time?"

"Emmaline, I advised you last time she got into trouble I would not be able to keep her out of trouble if she got into anything else. I am sworn by law to detain her until trial. This time is different from those other times. She was driving the car that was waiting for the other offenders when the owner had gotten shot and died on the floor of his General Store. Sarah will have to remain in jail and stand trial with the others for the death of the business owner."

"Oh, God!! Okay, I will be down sometime today to visit her."

"I am sorry Emmaline. I wish there were something more I could do to help."

"It is okay Sheriff. I understand."

*****

Pine Mountain was a small rural town that was a major stop for the Passenger Train of the time. A train that ran from Columbus to Pine Mountain. Back in the day the mountain was also a favorite visiting spot for vacationers who wanted to go camping but would rather go somewhere they could stay in a cabin and not on the ground, in a tent. Emmaline found she loved the new town and the people whose children attended the school where she had been hired as a fifth-grade teacher.

After two years in Pine Mountain, she married another teacher at the school. Together, they finished raising Emmaline's brother and sister. While she finished raising her siblings, Emmaline began her own family. She had always wanted a family of her own, and now, she found she was living the life she had always dreamed of having one day.

*****

Mark had resolved years before, after finishing high school, he was going to follow in his father's footsteps, his dad had gone into the Army just out of high school. Mark planned to do the same thing and start his career as soon after high school as he could. After serving his country he wanted to go into law enforcement somewhere in the United States. Mark knew what he wanted and how to get it, but he preferred to serve his country first. He was over the moon with the plans he had made for himself, and the way they were coming together. He was going to be the first police officer in his family and bring honor to the family who meant so much to him.

When he got to Pine Mountain, Mark did not know how he was going to like his new school or the people in it. He resolved from his first day there, he would make the most of his new surroundings. Mark did not know if he could make any friends or if he would be the hermit, he had been in Pike County. Mark felt he needed friends in his new school, but he did not know if he had the personality to form any close, lasting friendships. He had always been a little standoffish when it came to meeting new people.

BRIAN WILCHAIR

Brian Wilchair was born in August 1934. He had jet black hair and gorgeous, big blue eyes. His eyes were so light against his natural tanned skin everyone could see his eyes without looking for them. He found he was becoming a handsome, dangerous young man, needing no one to tell him of his good looks.

Brian's parents had raised him on the family farm in Pine Mountain, Georgia. His parents owned one of the largest family farms in the area. On one side of the large white plantation house was a pasture that would hold ten to fifteen horses on any given day. On the other side was the pool, tennis court, and inside the bottom floor of the house was the bowling alley. Anything Brian could have wanted to do on weekends, he could find just outside his bedroom door.

Brian had to let someone else do the work in the fields for his family. He never touched a hoe, a shovel, or a rake. The truth was he did not know what any of those tools looked like. Brian spent his childhood with a Nanny. He was always being sheltered from poverty and anyone any different from himself and his family. When he and the family traveled into town, if someone that was not as privileged as he was, walked up to the family, his parents would tell Brian they were beggars.

His family owned a large two-story antebellum house the Wilchar's had passed down for four generations before Brian was born. They had told the other large landowners' years before Brian would be the one to own the property one day. Him being the oldest put him in line to inherit the house and all the property when his parents passed away. His parents were Captain Abraham Wilchar and his lovely wife Abigail Rene' Pierce. They had raised their son to go to private schools and when he went into middle school; they sent him away to the military school nearby, but Brian decided he wanted to attend the local high school when he reached his freshman year.

When Brian began the ninth grade, he joined the local schools Jr. ROTC program and had already made plans to join the Army after graduation. During Brian's freshman year, he stayed to himself. Only friends he made were the guys in ROTC. If it had not been for those young men, he would have become a recluse that year. His parents were becoming concerned about him. They wondered if something else might be bothering Brian and that might be the reason; he had made no friends.

When school opened for the first day of school of his 10th grade year, Brian sat down beside a new young man in his class and the two young men began to talk.

"Hi, my name is Mark Mitchell."

"Hi, Mark nice to meet you, I am Brian Wilchar."

"Nice to meet you, Brian."

"How long have you lived in Pine Mountain?"

"I just moved here this summer."

"I am glad you did."

"How long have you lived here?"

"All of my life. My family owns the big farm that you can see from anywhere in town."

Brian and Mark became best friends that first day. They hit it off immediately. By the end of the day, they felt as though they had known each other their entire lives. Over the next year Brian helped Mark with his math homework, and in the process helped himself make better grades in math. While the two boys were doing their homework together, they began a friendship that would last them the rest of their lives. Even though they were from two different worlds, they formed a bond that a sibling could hope to have with their brother or sister. If one did something such as a school dance, ROTC, after-school activities of any kind the other would not be far away.

Before they graduated high school, they joined the Army. After graduation, both young men decided they wanted to see something of the world before they gave the military their lives. It was about two years later when they talked about their plans. They entered basic training at Fort Benning, Georgia. Both decided early in their lives to make the military their chosen profession and give of themselves as much as they could to their country.

When Brian and Mark graduated, they carried through with their plans to join the military. Both began their careers in the military at the rank of corporal. Even though the Army could not recruit them while they were in high school with the medals these two young men had earned for themselves over the years. They would be allowed to keep their ranks. Best of all they would be up for another promotion when they finished basic training.

Brian knew how far his parents and his last name could take him, but he wanted to make progress in his career on his own. At eighteen he enlisted in the Army. After basic training at Fort Benning, Georgia, the Department of Defense sent him to Fort

Knox to serve as his first duty station. Soon, they would send him back to Fort Benning for Ranger training. His commander in Kentucky saw a great deal of potential in Brian and wanted to get him into one of these classes as soon as he could.

His ROTC experience helped him get the appointments he wanted. After basic training military officials sent Brian and Mark to different duty stations, Brian was going to Kentucky to serve at Fort Knox to continue his sniper training. They stationed Mark at Fort Leavenworth where he could follow his love of law enforcement. After two years, they invited both young men to sign up for Ranger School at Fort Benning. Each commanding officer notified the Army that both Brian and Mark would like to apply for Ranger School that year. They knew they were lucky to get a letter of acceptance to any class at Fort Benning. Military officials had considered both for the first class but neither of them could attend. They would be a member of the second Class of Ranger School. Brain and Mark were to leave for Fort Benning in two weeks from two different posts in different parts of the United States.

Ranger School was a chance for both men to have the Military educate them so they could achieve what they had always dreamed about doing. Brian wanted to be a sniper with the Army and Mark was interested in police work. Experience these men got from Ranger Training could help them obtain their goals in their chosen Military career.

LACEY KACEY BURT

Lacey was born in Phenix City, Alabama in January 1935. Her family had lived in the same small house, her entire life. Lacey was one of those youngsters who enjoyed the infusion of cash from the ill-gotten gains of those sleazy businesses she always heard about existing downtown. She attended Central High School while those criminal enterprises were up and running, but she was oblivious to what kind of business was being conducted inside them. That kind of activity meant nothing to her, she was not a part of it so to her it never happened.

Lacey Burt was a nineteen-year-old tall, blond hair, blue-eyed beauty. When she walked across the stage to receive her diploma the year before it had been her opinion, she had the world at her feet. All she had to do was ask, and she could accomplish anything she set her mind.

She came to the realization really fast how the world really worked the day she began her search for a job. To her dismay, she was just one of many others looking for their first job. It was her intention to find a position that summer so she could help put herself through college. The University of Alabama mailed Lacey an admission letter two weeks after graduation. She received two scholarships from the University which she could use to pay for most of her education. Lacey wanted to at least have a start towards the money required to get her education.

Every business she applied with gave her the same excuse; you do not have sufficient experience. Well, if business owners are not prepared to give her the chance to fill one of these positions, she wondered how she could get the experience required to get and keep one of these honorable jobs. She applied with every reputable business in town for one of these positions, as her mother called them. But, to her dismay she could not find any kind of work she thought she could sink her teeth into. Lacey could not see herself as an individual who worked in the local mill or anything dealing with mechanical things. She thought she did not have the aptitude for that kind of work, and she overlooked taking any typing or any other business courses while in high school. Lacey wished now she had because with no skills it narrowed her choices of jobs for which she could qualify. If by some miracle she did luck up and get one, she would not have the experience to hold that job for long.

After a while, she understood why everyone always told her there were few positions in the Phenix City/Columbus area she was qualified for. Everybody always said what was available was at one of the local mills. Lacey did not want to work for one of them. She had several family members and friends who had found work there. She knew the money was okay, but not the best in the world. Lacey still insisted she did not want that type of work. Her parents brought her up with her mother working in the cotton mills and in her mind, she had a clear picture of what she wanted to do. Mill work, she came to realize, was not it. Even if it was for a year, maybe two.

After a few weeks, Lacey faced the same obstacle most of her friends had run into when they searched for their first job. Lacey felt as though she was a failure. All she wanted to do, all day, was stay in bed. Feeling down about not being able to find a position, as she was walking home from the last place she tried, Lacey bumped into one of her old friends from high school. Her friend mentioned to her a position, one of her friends had taken at the gambling house in town.

As Lacey stood there and listened to her friend describe what she was doing. Lacey let her mind drift to how she would tell her mother the details of the job her friend was describing. Lacey's friend was working as one of the "B-girls" at Ma Beachies Swing Time Club. Most of these B-girls met the men on the streets and enticed them into the bordello for a good time, or they might be able to interest them in some gambling for the evening.

Lacey would tell her parents the same thing other girls told their parents when they started at Ma's. Every girl who worked for Ma seemed to come up with the same story, they would be working as a hostess with a local restaurant. Only thing about this hostess job, it was inside Ma's bordello. Hostesses in 1953 were the cover jobs for girls working as local prostitutes. She did not see any alternative and this was not the kind of work Lacey had foreseen for herself. Lacey talked to every business in town and found there was not another job she could perform with her noticeable lack of experience. Every business in town told her "Come back when you have gotten the experience needed to do the job, she was asking employers to take a chance and hire her for."

Lacey's mom worked for the local mill all her life. Even with the degree, she had received from The University of Georgia she still found only work at the local mill available to her. Several of her family members worked in the mill with her. Lacey saw her mom slave away at the mill with the promise of getting only a paycheck. She loathed everything about that kind of work, the smell, the long hours, and even the risk some employees took with their health. Lacey's mom had come home several nights and told the family about someone who had lost a finger in one of the looms. One night she came home and told the story of how someone had lost their life when they fell off of the loom they were working on and landed in the one next to it while it was still running.

Lacey did not want to hurt her mother's feelings, but she did not want anything to do with this smelly, dangerous place. Every afternoon when her mother came in from work Lacey's face changed into some of the most distorted, grotesque shapes she thought people could ever imagine. To her, her mother smelled awful, and could not wait to get away from her, if only for a little while.

When Julie got home most afternoons, she ranted that everyone in the house felt as though they were too good to do the kind of work, she did. She had been throwing up to Lacey the last six weeks, she had it in her head that she was better than everybody else, including her. Lacey tried to talk to her mom and make her understand she did not think she had the mentality for working in one of the mills, but Julie wanted to hear nothing about Lacey's thoughts about the mill or what she could handle.

****

JULIE LACEY SINCLAIR

Julie was born in South Carolina in August 1903. She was the daughter of a South Carolina Representative. Her parents held everything Julie did to a higher standard than any of the other parents in town. All of Julie's actions and her friends were always being watched. If anyone wanted to be friends with her, they had to submit to a background check. Julie wanted away from her father, but she loved him and wanted to never disappoint him, on purpose.

When Julie was seven years old, the citizens of South Carolina elected her father to the State House for the first time. She spent most of her childhood in Columbia, South Carolina. Her parent's put every friend she had under a microscope. If one of them got into any kind of trouble Julie could never speak to them again.

As Julie grew and approached graduation she wanted, more than anything, to go away to college, but her father thought she should stay in South Carolina. He was pushing her to attend school there, but Julie had other ideas. Without telling him she had applied to the University of Georgia. Julie saw no reason to tell him about UGA before she was accepted. To her disbelief her letter came in the mail stating that Georgia had accepted her to the prestigious University. Now Julie had to face the fact that she had another problem, she had gone against her father's wishes, and he was going to be angry with her. She had never stood up to her father and did not know if she could find the courage to tell him she was going out of the State of South Carolina to go to college.

Julie was to begin her college career at the University of Georgia in a few weeks. She had promised herself she would tell her father before the summer was over, and summer was fast coming to an end, September was only two weeks away. Now she had to find the nerve to tell her him about what she had decided to do. Julie had put off telling him her news the entire summer. She had known for two weeks she was running out of time before she had to face the consequences of her decision. The University of Georgia admissions schedule made it necessary for her to leave South Carolina and arrive in Athens, Georgia in a few days. With this new development it became necessary for her to tell her father immediately. That afternoon Julie, asked her dad if he would like to take a walk with her, giving them some time alone so she could tell him her news. As they walked, Julie broke the news to him.

"Daddy, I am not going to Clemson. I have decided to go to the University of Georgia."

"What do you mean?"

"I have decided, I want to go to the University of Georgia. I need some time away from home. I want to learn to take care of myself."

"You know, for many generations, everyone in our family has gone to Clemson."

"I am sorry, Daddy, but I want to go to Georgia."

When they finished talking, Julie walked back to the house alone. Her father would not talk to Julie, she had upset him. All he wanted, now, was to walk the property alone and have some time to think. After about an hour, he returned, but he did not speak to her again. Her mother made plans for Julie to leave for Athens the next afternoon. As she was packing her car, she could see her father watching from the window in his study. As she drove off, he had not come down from his bedroom to see her. To her dismay as she pulled out of the driveway, he never waved to her and when he noticed her looking at him from the road, he pulled the curtains.

After Julie moved to Athens, she did not see much of her parents. She always found something to do on campus or with friends during spring and Christmas breaks, and between quarters. Her father never forgave Julie for choosing to attend Georgia. He was a Clemson alumni and wanted his daughter to continue the family tradition. Julie had to live with the fact that her father saw her as someone who had abandoned family tradition, he never forgave her for this and the two of them never spoke again. When Julie began at Georgia, she met, in her freshman year, a sophomore named John Anthony Burt.

****

JOHN ANTHONY BURT

John was a good-looking young man who played football at the University of Georgia as a defensive lineman. So, he had to keep himself in shape and with his six foot five inches he had enough muscle to help the team and still not be overweight. After football season John and Julie became inseparable. John was always working out, trying to get stronger and better for the next football season. After he met Julie, he would spend as much of his time with her as he could. He would not jeopardize his status with the football team, but he had fallen hard for Julie Sinclair.

Julie attended classes during the summer, allowing her to earn the credits she needed to be eligible to graduate the same year as John. After graduation, both got jobs in Columbus, Georgia. Julie found them a house in Phenix City, Alabama that was right for a family who was beginning their lives together. Before they left Athens, John and Julie had invited their friends and family to their wedding. As young people they wanted to be married before they started their lives together leaving them the ability to start their lives with clean slates. With their reputations and friends, not their parents making their way in life for them.

John's family attended their son's wedding. His parents welcomed their new daughter-in-law into the family with open arms. Julie had mailed her parents an invitation to her wedding and called her mother to ask them to come.

Her mother told her,

"You know how your father gets when his wishes are not considered or followed to the letter."

"Yes, Mom, I know how he gets. Is he still holding it against me that I chose Georgia and not Clemson?"

"Yes, you know you hurt him when you decided to go out of State to College."

"Will he ever forgive me?"

"I cannot speak for him, but I do not see it happening anytime soon, if ever."

"Okay, I love you, Mom."

"I love you, too."

****

John and Julie welcomed their first child in March 1929. Their first-born was a son they named after John, John Anthony Burt, Jr. came screaming into their lives on March 8, 1929. John Anthony Burt, Jr. grew up with an interest in law enforcement and a desire to help people. Tony wanted to keep his neighborhood safe. To follow his dreams, he too attended the University of Georgia. When he returned home, he found employment with the city. In his positions with the city, he would witness some of the worst violence he could have dreamed could happen to a person. There was no way he could ever forget the horrors he had seen. People could do some of the most unspeakable things to other people. It was at times as though they had no soul, and no compassion for their fellow man.

During the violence in Phenix City, Tony would be one of the officers who would help shut down the illegal businesses that were being ignored by local law enforcement. He would be one of two individuals who found his sister's boyfriend after his brutal murder. He was the person who stumbled over Brian's beaten body. A body they had just left lying in Holland Creek like a piece of trash after Ma Beachies enforcers left him that June night. Tony's partner had caught him before he could fall on Brian's lifeless body.

****

In 1931 on Valentine's Day, Andrew Johnson Burt was born. Andy would be the total opposite of Tony. He was always in some kind of trouble. Nothing his parents did would make Andy understand his actions would one day have dire consequences.

Andy in 1950 decided he did not want to go to college. He wanted to go to work straight out of high school. Able to find work as soon as he went into town with Ma Beachies. Ma gave him the cover story to tell his parents his duties were that of a bouncer. He was to take care of the clients that were in the lounge of her new establishment.

****

On Christmas Day in 1932, Lacey's sister, Justine Maria Burt was born. She was a delightful young woman from the moment she entered this life. Justie was trying to look after her siblings. Some of her siblings, she discovered early in life, she could not save. They were out of control even at an early age.

Justie attended the University of Alabama for four years. She was in hopes she would accomplish her dream of getting her college degree and go into Social Work. Social work had become her dream when she found that had a desire to help people, old and young alike. She could not believe the terrible atrocities that

35

these two sections of the population had to endure just to get by in life.

While she was in Tuscaloosa, she joined a Sorority. In 1952 joining sororities was an excellent step to get ahead, in any career and to find a husband. Justie would use her degree as a steppingstone to advance her knowledge and develop into what she wanted to do. She wanted to be a good Social Worker. By seeking to benefit needy kids and the aged who were being mistreated at a dangerous rate. Both groups needed help more than her professors ever led her or any of their students to believe as a true issue. After four years, Justie finished her degree and set out to accomplish her dreams on her own.

****

On June 10, 1936, Lacey's baby sister entered her life, Jennifer Rebecca Burt was a daddy's girl from the second she was born. She was always John's baby, and in his eyes, she could do no wrong. Life in the Burt household became hard for the other children to deal with, and the younger ones developed behavioral issues.

Becky would go on to college, two years, after she graduated from high school. There was a new college founded in Columbus that she attended for four years. During her four years at Columbus College, Becky was a fantastic student in her chosen line of work. She achieved a 4.0-grade point average. When the time for graduation from Columbus College came, she had earned a degree in Education. Most of Becky's family wanted her to become a teacher at one of the high schools in town. It was a happy occasion when in less than a year, she had found her dream job at Hardaway High School, and her parents were pleased that she would not be going far from home to make her life.

LACEY MEETS MA BEACHIES

L acey got up early the next morning strolled downtown to apply for work with Ma Beachies. When they laid eyes on her blonde hair and beautiful face everyone there fell in love with her. Taken with her they gave her the lecture everyone gets when they work for Ma and given the required time for her to start her new job that Friday night. As part of her orientation, they warned Lacey what the repercussions would be if she fell in love or socialized with clients outside of Ma's. Lacey was to have no contact with any of the men who came to enjoy her company at Ma Beachies place. And one day like Him I will be!

She had found a good-paying job, but it was not anything like what she had wanted. Lacey would work every Friday and Saturday night. She found however she was scared to tell her parents what she was going to be doing. Some things they told her was part of her job was a little on the illegal side of the law. Even in Phenix City, but her boss and some of the other business owners owned and ran Phenix City.

She was the type men liked to see when they got off from work for the weekend or got leave from the base. She was high spirited, and a lot of fun to be around. Being one of the girls who was lucky enough to work those two nights she made as much or more than the girls who worked the rest of the week.

It would be one of these Friday nights when Brian and Mark each met Lacey. Neither one ever came in when the other was in Ma Beachies Swing Time Club. As fate would have it, they were both seeing the same blonde hair beauty at Ma Beachies.

Brian Wilchair was one of Lacey's first customers that first Friday night. During her first encounter with him, Ma had instructed her to show Brian a fun time, both in a sexual and personal nature. When they finished upstairs, she was to take him to the gambling room in the back for a little of the other action Ma had going on. During their first meeting, Lacey did as they instructed her, to a point.

She and Brian spent an hour in her room. On this first night, she was reluctant to do anything with him except talk. Lacey could feel the heat between them from the moment they met. She caught him staring at her which made her blush.

"What's that all about?"

"I like you, Brian. I do not want to ruin it by giving you the wrong impression of me."

"But we just met."

"I know, but there is something special about you."

All they did that first night was sit and talk. He paid her what Ma had told him the hour of her time was worth. After an hour, Lacey showed him to the gambling room. He would stay there the rest of the night. Occasionally, Lacey would come back in and sit down beside him for luck. That first night she seemed to help because he walked out of there with a pot load of money.

ANDY AND LACEY TALK

Andy had recognized his sister the moment she walked into the Swing Time Club. He met his sister at the door of the family home the second she got home.

"Lacey, we need to talk."

"What about Andy."

"Did you know that I am one of the bouncers at Ma's?"

"No, but Andy this is my decision, not yours."

"Lacey, I do not want anything to happen to you but you are playing with something here that you may not know how to handle."

"Are you going to tell Mom and Dad?"

"No, are you going to tell them what I am doing?"

"Andy that is your business you are a grown man, if you want to work for Ma and do the job, she has asked you to do, that is your business, not mine."

"Thank you, Lacey, I love you, and I don't want to see you hurt."

"As long as we follow the rules, we will be fine. Don't you think we can work together and keep the fact that you are my brother between us?"

"Ma already knows you are my sister, and as long as I don't play favorites everything is good with her. I think you should know; I was the one that asked her to give you the job."

"What, thank you."

After that Andy walked off and left Lacey standing there alone. She could not believe her bother had done that for her. He knew the risk they were taking but he wanted to help her find a job and a way to take care of herself for a change.

MA BEACHIES SWING TIME CLUB

Ma Beachie was born Breachia Revely "Beachie" Brigman, March 19, 1891. As she grew up, Ma had always been short, she reached a height of five feet one inches. It was to Ma's benefit everyone in town knew her. Ma had married a man, together they moved to New Orleans, and learned the ways of running a night club the Cajun way. When she returned to Phenix City, after her husband's death, she put that knowledge she had obtained while she was gone to good use, and opened her own night club which she called, Ma Beachies Swing Time Club.

Everyone in town thought of her as a grandmotherly figure, and around town it was a well-known fact she had guns in her place of business. It was even thought she kept two pistols under the bar where she sat. She had no problem using them on anyone who came in wanting to start trouble. It did not matter to her or anyone else she might weigh one hundred pounds soaking wet. She was slight in stature, but she had a way of making men do whatever she wanted. Women would peddle their bodies for her. When people saw her, they could not believe she could possess that much sway. None of the officials in Montgomery or even the Dixie Mafia thought she could control men in the city government, get them on her payroll, and in a position to do her bidding. To everyone's amazement she could wrap people around her little finger quicker than using any amount of honey.

She might be a small-framed woman, but her reputation made her seem to be a lot larger. Ma faced demons of her own. Her past caused her great sorrow, one night, while she was in the backroom conducting the nightly business of the Swing Club, her daughter, Goldie, died upstairs in 1948 of a drug overdose. Many of those who worked for the local newspaper reported Goldie was a drug addict. Some who had ties to the newspaper ran the story of how they discovered her body. To Ma's horror they also reported some of the details surrounding her daughter's death and where she was found.

When Goldie was found during the night. Ma had to change the way she did business while the police and investigators were inside the Swing Club. It was of no help that most of the police force, sheriff's office and city hall were on her payroll, with the newspaper reporters coming by about every hour to see what the latest information might have brought to light. All this attention made it necessary for Ma to give her place a distinctive look and feel that was different from the normal atmosphere men had grown accustomed to enjoying any other night. Ma was not too afraid that the newspaper might find out the truth about her club, she knew that if they got too close the Dixie Mafia would take care of the problem before it could get out of hand.

On a normal night it was according to which type of young woman you had a hankering to be with, the charge for an hour with her could be $5. That is if all you required was a little companionship for about an hour you could get it with little effort. If you were searching for a night of passion and real fun that would cost, you $50. Ma allowed her girls to be with men who could pay the steeper prices. Ma knew these men were of a quality that was above reproach. Ma and the head bouncer made sure everyone was showing the gentlemen a good time, and they would take care of them and the business to the standard Ma had set.

In Phenix City, if you were in the mood for shady women, you could find a prostitute on every corner. Gambling was also in the houses, but they had to hide the machines a little better. Business owners would set each of their houses up in the same style. When you stepped into the primary entrance, the first thing you saw was the bar. If the bartender did not recognize you as a police officer, all a client needed to do was ask, and walk into the Club. Nobody ever said anything to you after that except, "how would like to spend your night. We have a wide variety, and we know for sure one of them will strike your fancy."

After showing the men a brief interlude with ecstasy, the young women took the men back downstairs. Tables inside Ma's Swing Time Club were said by patrons as being honest until about 1:00 a.m. After that, all bets were off if you came in from upstairs you would find out the hard way that you could walk out of there with nothing or even lose your life. Most of the men who did win did so with Ma's endorsement.

MEET THE OTHER PLAYERS BOOTLEGGING – IN THE SOUTH

Ma Beachies and Hoyt Shepherd still brewed and distributed illegal alcohol from their downtown offices on Friday and Saturday nights. Both believed no one could do anything to them. They were convinced they had paid everyone off so they could do as they pleased. It was a known fact they were part of the Dixie Mafia and had their protection. No one dared go against this group if they wanted to see another day. Hoyt being the head of The Machine in Phenix City gave he and Ma an advantage. They could do anything they wanted in town.

Bootleggers ran alcohol from and through Phenix City. These trips usually began at Ma or Hoyt's front door. They hired experienced men to carry out the runs on weekends. Men, they knew would travel routes out of their way before they headed towards their designated destinations. A few of the bootleggers would get to the Alabama-Tennessee line before they would get arrested with their illegal cargo. Most of the time these drivers had no idea what they were carrying in the trunk of their cars. When local sheriffs confiscated the merchandise, these inexperienced drivers cost Ma and Hoyt hundreds of dollars. Ma and Hoyt had bootlegged alcohol into town for the resident's consumption since before the federal government repelled prohibition. Ma would bring in men to drive their cars, deliver the whiskey they made during the week. Ma ran her business from her office at Ma Beachies Swing Time Club. Everyone who wanted to drive for her, or Hoyt would go to her office to ask for an assignment. Ma always had a pile of applications for drivers she could go through and find someone new no one would be looking for on Friday or Saturday night.

Most Friday mornings you would find Ma in her office going through this stack of applications. She would search for an individual she liked to run her alcohol to Tennessee, Texas, Mississippi, or even Oklahoma. Ma had gained the reputation of being clairvoyant with the use of drivers who would get the merchandise through no matter who was chasing her cars through the perilous roads between Phenix City and all points north and west. They drove through mountain roads that were no bigger than goat trails. So, whoever drove each week might come back in one piece and some of them might come back in a pine box. There had been several who drove off the mountain in Tennessee and wasted their entire load. Most of the time the newcomer drivers were hauling a decoy load so the cars with the moonshine could get through undetected.

This weekend Ma decided on an experienced fellow out of Shiloh, Georgia. He was a tall, good-looking young man. In the face, he caused people to think of Hank Williams, but he had nerves of steel. Larry Hearn had driven for Ma on more than one occasion and was one man she wanted to take her alcohol to Arkansas and Tennessee. He arrived alive, and the shipment still in one piece, no matter who was chasing him.

The Machine knew they had two men who could get their merchandise through and when a purchaser had bought a product that was a little better than usual. Ma and Hoyt would call upon those two men when they wanted their product to the purchaser on time and without any excitement along the way.

They had intended to use decoys for the shipment that Friday night. They were moving this shipment to Vicksburg,

Mississippi. Both Ma and Hoyt would try a little bait and switch to determine if they could not get their precious freight through to the purchaser in

Tennessee. They had realized this job would require someone who could get the merchandise to the buyer and avoid roadblocks, drive on backwoods roads, and make the adjustments to the routes and keep their time schedules. They had to do all this while staying one step ahead of the backwoods sheriffs.

Different counties brought in law enforcers to travel the back roads of the county bootleggers were known to run each Friday night. They disclosed to the men who were carrying out the deliveries they had precious gems in the rear of their cars. These drivers had no idea they had moonshine in their trunks. Nobody pointed out to them there was some more illegal merchandise hidden in with their cargo. There was a considerable bonus waiting at the end of the run for the driver who delivered their freight to its destination in one piece and without the man getting caught.

Ma called Larry to drive for her this week, and he admitted he liked the idea of his running the order to her connection in Arkansas. On Thursday afternoon, Larry visited Ma Beachies to get the details about the next nights delivery. As she gave him the envelope full of money, and the route he was to take that night. He noticed Ma staring at him. She never took the time before to worry about one driver or to even speculate how someone could get through various parts of the route and others could not.

After work that Friday afternoon, Larry went to the address he had been given to pick up his hot load. As they loaded the alcohol, he walked into the backroom to use the restroom. While he was in the back, he saw the pictures of the other men who had run alcohol for them for the last three weeks. He had no idea where Ma had gotten the pictures that hung on her wall. Larry could not imagine someone could have enough pull to get whatever they wanted from the police in the State they had demolished their car and lost their valuable load.

With the pictures, he had seen hanging on the wall when he walked into the hall leading to the restroom. Those pictures were still stuck in his head, as he walked back into the garage where Ma's men were completing the loading of the alcohol for this weekend's run. As they were putting the trunk back onto the car, Larry stood there and let the memory of the pictures he had seen on the wall in the back-office sink into his memory.

As he pulled out of the garage, he marveled at how lucky he had been to never have gotten into a situation like that. Larry realized he had been down those same roads on many trips before. He never knew when he might make a mistake and wind-up upside down in a ditch somewhere. Larry got the feeling he had been lucky and wondered when his luck might run out.

But, not this weekend, he was going nowhere near the Tennessee roads and mountains. His trip was one that he had made many times before and there were no mountains he had to run through. The trip to Arkansas was almost flat, but with these trips, you never knew what to expect from one minute to the next.

Larry started his trip about 9:00 p.m. that Friday night. He had to be in Little Rock, Arkansas by 10:00 p.m. the next night. Larry always tried to get some sleep during the day in some out of the way cove and complete his run and deliver by the designated time.

He was not new to Ma, and she knew she could trust him to complete his run. He was about three hours into his run when someone in a diner he stopped to eat every time he made one of these runs thought they knew him. Larry noticed a sheriff's deputy sitting at the bar when the man announced his name. Larry sat down, ordered his dinner, and ate his meal before paying the waitress, and turning to leave. When he stepped out of the diner, got into his car, and began the rest of the trip to Little Rock, he decided he would take a route he had never traveled before.

Larry did not let on that he knew the man in the diner, or that he overheard the deputy radio dispatch. They informed the deputy they were sending some help to intercept him before he got into Little Rock. As he walked out of the diner, Larry overheard the sheriff talking on the radio he had locked in his car. No one had any idea that Larry had been lucky enough to overhear the conversation. So, as he drove out of the parking lot to keep anyone from suspecting he knew what they were planning he turned on the road with a direct route to Little Rock. When Larry got out of sight of the diner, he turned down another road that headed into Little Rock. None of the people who were used to set up the roadblocks ever saw him go through any of them.

When Larry brought himself and his car back into Phenix City that Sunday night, he handed Ma the money for the alcohol and received his pay. He informed her that someone recognized him when he stopped to eat, but he had dealt with the situation. Larry realized the only way someone could have identified him was that someone had reported what was in his car to the authorities in that area. He suspected Ma had been the one to call Little Rock and have someone from the sheriff's office waiting on him. He kept his options open for the next time someone contacted him for a run for Ma and Hoyt Sheppard, but in his heart, he knew that was his last run.

ALEX AND ANDY'S JOB

Alexander Benjamin Mitchell came to Phenix City after his discharge from the Army. He had been in the small town for two weeks before he was able to find a job. A job made it possible for him to stay in town and take care of himself. Alex worried many nights if he was going to be able to find any work in the small town at all. He was happy when given any chance to prove himself. Any position he wanted required the experience would have the need for a law enforcement background. Alex, since the day he enlisted in the Army, worked out every day to refine his muscles. All the exercise they made him do in the Army made his muscles more defined. His body made the women act as if they had never been in the presence of a well-built man before. Anyone of them would tell everyone they were lucky to be with him. Women loved to stare at Alex's body. Most women thought of him as though he was a living god. In the last couple of years, he made it a point to work on his stomach muscles. Really define the muscles of his abdomen because he wanted the women to fawn over him. He was a little vein as well; he liked the way his body looked, and the way women fawned over him because of it.

When his parents were suddenly taken in a tragic accident a classmate from Concord came to Ma's to tell him about their death. His sister never picked up the phone to let him know the details of their death. As far as her siblings were aware, Emmaline did not have another brother, she stopped claiming Alex years before he left home. Alex and Emmaline had gotten into a huge argument, and they exchanged words that neither one of them ever intended on taking back. It still hurt both to think of the way they left things all those years ago, but they had no intention of making up now.

When Alex decided to go to the funeral, he wondered if anyone would recognize him. It had been a long time, and when Alex showed up at the funeral, his sister treated him as a stranger and gave him the cold shoulder. He had no choice but to remain to himself in the sanctuary's rear. In his sister's eyes, he had always been the outcast of the family, and nobody had ever spoken of him around the younger children. Alex believed none of them even knew they had an older brother. So, he left it that way, or so he thought. Alex never had any idea that Mark did remember him.

To keep down the possibility of an argument, at the cemetery, he stood under a tree and listened to the service for his parents while everyone else stood with the family. None of the other siblings ever knew he had attended their parents' funeral. If anyone of the younger children had seen him there, they would have no idea who he was. Emmaline knew he was there, but she said nothing to him. She had noticed him a couple times during the day, once in the sanctuary and then again standing under the tree listening to the service, It made everyone sad though, the younger kids had no idea they had another brother. As far as Emmaline was concerned, she did not have another brother and wanted none of her siblings to suspect he was anywhere near the cemetery that afternoon.

Neither Alex nor Emmaline knew that Mark had seen him standing there. Mark remembered his older brother from the time he had spent with him before he went into the army. He vowed he would get know his older brother, someday.

*****

Andrew Johnson Burt still lived with his parents when Phenix City first gained the honor of being called the first "Sin City." His friends told him about an establishment that hired bodyguards for Ma Beachies Swing Time Club. He got up out of his cozy bed the next morning, walked to the club, and applied for a position as a bouncer. With the look of his body, he landed a position on the spot. No one realized the other title he carried. He was second in command of those Ma called her Enforcers. These were the Bouncers loyal to her and would reveal to no one any of her secrets. Ma trusted these two handsome, young men above all others.

Alex and Andy, in the time they had worked for Ma, became best friends. They had met when they both were in Ma's office applying for employment with Ma two years before. On weekdays, anybody who needed to find Ma Beachies bouncers could find them in the gym in the rear of Ma Beachies place working out to keep themselves in shape. On Friday and on weekends one of them would be in the main gambling room while they would position the other so no one would realize they were there. If something developed, and the other needed aid, men would come out of every corner of Ma Beachies place. There was more protection in that house than there was on the streets of Phenix City.

After 1:00 a.m. it is not obvious who needed protecting the house or the clients. They would roll most clients who were in the house that late on their way out the door. No one was above the treatment. They rigged even the roulette table to take all your cash and give it back to the house. Ma's was rumored to be legal until after 1:00 a.m. by patrons who knew what was happening inside the gambling houses and clubs during the days of "Sin City."

Soldiers who came in for a suitable time stayed past 1:00 a.m. Military leaders ordered those who arrived for basic training to stay out of Phenix City. None of them seemed to take notice because every Friday and Saturday night you could find the soldiers from Fort Benning at Ma Beachies Swing Time Club or the Blue Bonnet.

They had heard about the women and gambling available on any given night in Phenix City. Many of them wanted to know what the big deal was about going to this city. Why did the officers have such an issue with Phenix City? There was so much talk about the city that everybody wanted to know what was going on. With no one being immune from the draws of Phenix City. Anyone could find a good time, even men twice the soldiers age in these clubs on Friday and Saturday night. These men, all, came in for a good time and to do a little gambling. Many had the hopes of hitting it big and being able to take care of their families and homes just a little better.

BRIAN – RANGER TRAINING

His parents had raised Brian in a small backwoods town that sat at the top of what people in the area call a mountain. This picturesque town is about a thirty minute drive northeast of Columbus, Georgia. His family home was nestled in a town called Pine Mountain. Brian made several friends who lived in Phenix City while he attended Military School in another small town called Dadeville, Alabama. None of his friends ever said anything to him about the kind of cruelty that was taking place right under their noses in the town they called home. Brian realized a long time ago he was a person who lived for the surge of adrenaline. He loved the way his body felt when he was in a position that could become life-threatening at a moment's notice. He was always up to a proper round of chicken with his car or a game of poker with his friends on any given night.

Brian enlisted in the Army and began basic training as a sergeant at Fort Benning. He remembered a few of his friends at Fort Knox telling him stories about the fun young men could find across the river. Stories which included tales of women, gambling, and if he could find a fast car, he could make some serious money running alcohol on Friday and Saturday. During basic training none of his friends mentioned what was going on in the town that rests just across the river. Brian and Mark had completed basic training at Fort Benning two years before and were looking forward to seeing the old place again. At least, Brian was. He did not know how Mark felt about being back in Phenix City, he had not spoken to Mark in two months.

When he left Columbus and Fort Benning, army officials assigned him to Fort Knox, Kentucky to strengthen his career with the Army. His desire for an army career differed from every other male, he requested to be put into the infantry but because of his family; they assigned him a desk job in Kentucky. His job was to protect the country's gold reserve. Not the position he sought but officials viewed this assignment as appropriate for him. Whatever, Brian's father asked them to do they were glad to do for their old friend.

Brian spent two years at this duty station and realized he wanted more. To him protecting the gold reserve was too mundane. Brian loved the rush that came with doing something dangerous and exciting. He was becoming bored with doing the same thing day after day. So, he went and spoke to his commanding officer about what he wanted from his military career. He and his commanding officer were well aware the only way he would get to do more for his country than look after the country's gold supply. He would have to get some kind of specialized training. Brian wanted to tour other countries and be a part of keeping his country secure, not watch his friends see all the places he had seen while he was growing up.

He was aware his father was pulling the strings concerning his career. Brian wanted to take control of his own life and see a little of the action. He had a plan in mind and wrote letters to the commanding officer of Ranger School. He was ready and if they still had space for him, he was ready to attend.

Fort Benning had contacted him, every couple of weeks for over a year, army officials wanted him to be a part of the second class to graduate from their new Ranger program. Brian found the proposition an intriguing one. He approached his commanding officer to request more information talking about the program. Brian needed to learn what the program asked those who took part to give of themselves. How many who had begun the program finished the previous year. The base had contacted him to be in that first class, but he and his commanding officer could not figure out a way for him to complete his tour of duty that would allow him to accept their invitation. It was with a sad heart that he had to turn down their offer allowing him to take part in that first class. Brian was eager to get some kind of specialized training and had given his word that he would take part in a later class of Ranger School. With the Army only giving this opportunity to its better officer candidates during any rotation.

Every time someone spoke about Ranger school at Fort Benning Brian listened with a sense of awe and an attentive ear. He was getting the details of the new program and Brian liked the sound of the stamina that the course demanded for candidates to complete the rigorous training. He was curious about the kind of training he would receive and would do more investigation of his own into what being one of these rangers would mean to the United States in years to come. As far as he was concerned, though, he wanted the prestige that seemed to go with being one of these Rangers. He knew it would make his father happy and nothing would please Brian Wilchar more than to make his father proud. Not to mention it was something Brian could claim as his own and not share with his father. When his dad had gone through basic and entered his military career, there was no such thing as a Ranger.

That afternoon, after supper, he called Mark to see if he had heard of this new program. Astonished by what his friend was asking him. He had a rough time getting the words out of his mouth.

"Brian, my CO asked today as well if I would like to be a part of this second group."

"What did you say?"

"I told them I would be proud, and it would be a great honor to be included in their second class."

"Well, then I will tell them I want to do it even more since you will be there as well. I did not want to do this course without someone to help me and enjoy it with."

"Good, we will be back together."

"See you in about two weeks."

"Okay, I cannot wait."

"Talk later."

"Bye."

Brian informed his commanding officer he would be honored to accept the opportunity he was being offered. It thrilled his commander when Brian decided to go through the training this time around. This would be a plus on his record and he knew Brian had the talent to do whatever he wanted if he put his mind to it.

After Brian accepted the offer to the Rangers, he took the liberty he had accumulated. Liberty gave him the chance to go to France, England, and Italy. As he was traveling through Paris; he went to the Eiffel Tower one more time, Lascaux's for its ancient cave drawings, and Lyon for their Roman theater. These places plus the great Palace of Versailles attest to the vivid past of the French countryside. In England, he decided he wanted to go to London, Wales, and Scotland. Most of his family had come from this area. When he had seen everything in England he wanted to visit, Brian packed his bags and boarded a plane headed to Italy. In the next week, he saw its capital, Rome, home to the Vatican and landmark art and ancient ruins. Other major cities include Florence, with Renaissance masterpieces such as Michelangelo's "David" and Brunelleschi's Duomo; Venice, the city of canals; and Milan, Italy's fashion capital.

When Brian returned to the States, he was to board a bus headed to Columbus, Georgia. He could not wait to see his old friend again. Brian was tired of being in strange towns alone. At least for a few months he would have somebody to talk to and enjoy his personal time with. You know, two can get into a lot more trouble than one and it is a lot more fun to have someone to enjoy it with.

MARK – RANGER TRAINING

Mark Mitchell came from a family that was dirt poor. He was the baby of the family and did not remember the tough times of the 1930s. Mark graduated from high school with honors and as far as he could tell a bright future lay ahead of him. He and Brian graduated at the top of their class from Pine Mountain High School.

Brian graduated as Valedictorian and Mark was Salutatorian of their senior class. They had gotten each other through high school one needed help with classes and the other with his own identity crisis. Brian might have come from a prominent family, but when Mark came to Pine Mountain Brian was having problems fitting in. Mark came along at a time in Brian's life where he needed a friend and Mark needed to feel as though he was impacting someone's life positively. Two weeks after graduation Mark decided he was going to hang around Pine Mountain for the summer. He found himself a job at the local swimming pool. Women who wanted to date him thought he was the best-looking guy they had ever seen. Two young girls tried to fake drowning just so Mark would jump in the pool and save them. In the afternoons after work, he found there was nothing else to do but sit and read.

During the summer before Mark joined the Army, he traveled home at night and helped his sister with her small children. She was the only parent he had ever known. He had been young when his parents had their accident and died. Mark was old enough to remember his parents, but their memory was fading fast. He knew in a few years he would not remember them at all.

He did not remember a lot about some of his siblings. Most of them had left home before he was old enough to remember who they were or what they looked like. Mark had not gotten the opportunity to form a lot of memories of most of his older siblings, just his sister. He was aware that if he were lucky enough to ever meet one of them on the street, he would not know who they were.

Mark had decided he was going to buy himself a house and build a home in Phenix City when his tour of duty was over. He had fallen in love with the quaint town when the army recruiters stationed him there for basic training two years before. Mark had no idea what he was in store for when he returned to the town, but it overjoyed him to have the chance to go back to a town he had made so many good memories.

When he arrived, he was going to find a house on the Phenix City side of the Chattahoochee River that he wanted to settle down in. He was going to put a down payment on the property. Mark would have a place to come back to when he got out of the army. He was putting down roots for himself during that summer. Mark wanted to find a wife and have a family of his own, someday. First, though he wanted to get through Ranger training, go to Korea, and come back to the States to follow his dreams of Law Enforcement either with the Army or with local police or sheriff's departments.

Mark had left Fort Benning as a Corporal when the army sent him at Fort Leavenworth. His duties in Kansas had been as a guard at the prison. Mark received several promotions and was now in charge of the military police at the Fort. Mark found his current duties satisfying because that was the kind of work, he had always dreamed of being a part of.

After a while, he found he wanted to do more with his life. He preferred to help those that could not help themselves. Mark was savoring his time in Kansas, but when the opportunity arose for him to go to Ranger school at Fort Benning, he jumped at the chance. What made the prospect of returning to Fort Benning so much more appealing to him was the thought of his getting to go home. When the call from Brian came telling him they had likewise extended him the invitation to go through the training, he was even more excited to be going back to the town he would eventually call home.

Mark got up early, he had packed his belongings the night before. He put on his uniform and got ready to go to the bus station. After he ate breakfast, his commanding officer came by and offered to take him to the station where he was to start his long trip to Columbus. It was going to take him two days to travel from Kansas to Georgia. He was more than ready for a change of scenery and traveling home sounded like just what he needed.

When his bus got into Columbus, another bus pulled ahead of his. Mark could not be more than two minutes ahead of Brian. Brian rode the bus from Kentucky and Mark sat in his seat looking for Brian to step off the bus. As Mark got off the bus, he walked over to the other bus to look for his friend. He wanted to see him and get caught up. They could sit and talk for a little while before they had to check in on base.

Mark waited the longest few minutes he thought he had ever experienced for Brian to get off the bus. The two old friends walked up to each other and pulled each other into a big hug. They walked over to the luggage compartment to get their bags out from under the bus. As they were walking through the bus station, they could not help but sit down and talk about old times and how glad they were to see each other. They got so caught up with catching up they almost forgot where they were and where they were going. Each of their commanding officers scheduled them to be on base at a certain time and they dare not be late. Both suddenly remembered they were to be on base in less than an hour. Mark called them a cab and when it arrived, they both got into the car.

As they were going through the gate, they could not believe how much the place had changed in only two years. The base had gotten a facelift in some areas and how much the old place had stayed the same. They felt as though they were coming home. When the two young men got out of the car, they took their belongings and walked into the barracks. Officers in charge of the training had assigned them their quarters when they spoke with the base to accept the invitation. As they walked into the barracks, they discovered that eight other men were already there. They were the rest of the class for that term. When they found their bunks, they got ready for bed to try to get some rest while they waited for their adventure to begin early the next day.

GOVERNMENT AGENTS

Informants told stories to agents of rooms with gambling of all sorts in them; roulette wheels, one arm bandits, poker, and twenty-one. Any game an individual could dream of was being carried out within the city limits. With no one trying to do away with the illegal ventures, this activity would go on as long as the citizens of Phenix City would tolerate these businesses. This environment had been going unchecked for a long time. Much of the crime would continue under the okay of the local sheriff and police chief until someone got hurt and the state could no longer tolerate the reputation Phenix City was giving the rest of the State.

Agents who were assigned to conduct inquiries into the business dealings in Phenix City reported back to their supervisors what agents before them had said they found. To other Attorney Generals, it sounded like a retelling of the first agents report, but not the AG of Alabama. Attorney General Si Garrett knew exactly what was going on in Phenix City, he was part of it.

When the governor sent another agent, who would spend the afternoon at Ma's writing about his stay he came to the same conclusion. None of the agents the governor had sent over the last few months could find anything else going on inside any of these businesses. Agents reported back to Montgomery, "they could not figure out what the citizens were so concerned about." That was the whole story, or as much of the story as Agents felt comfortable reporting back to Montgomery. There was not enough evidence to pinpoint what kind of shady activities were going on in Phenix City or if the citizens were just making the stories up to try to get attention from the state.

One agent who had been sent to gather evidence of the wrongs happening in Phenix City came back with a version of events that surprised everyone. Agents had been aware they were close to getting the evidence they needed but no one ever suspected just how close they were. Somehow, with this agent Ma had figured out who he was when she greeted him, but she still introduced him to one of her girls. She told the young lady to take her time, she needed to hide the other criminal activities before someone showed him what really happened at Ma Beachies Swing Time Club.

Officials in Montgomery were reluctant to assign any further agents to go into the small town. They wanted to try to get a handle on the lawless activity's citizens continued, daily, to send them letters about. Letters which described in detail the various crimes that had been going there for years. Montgomery could not figure out what was happening with their agents when they got to Phenix City, but they knew something was not right with the reports they were getting when agents returned. All the reports read too much alike. ABI agents knew something was happening with their agents, but no one could or would talk about what had happened to them while they were in town. It was up to the Alabama Bureau of Investigation to find a way to prove what was happening in the Central Alabama town, and prove what citizens, preachers, and the Russell Betterment Association had been telling them for years.

Things began to change when the new governor was elected. Governor Persons had every intention of making some kind of change in Phenix City. He wanted to help the citizens of the small town along the banks of the Chattahoochee River feel safe in their homes and to be able to walk down the street without fearing for their lives. Persons decided to send undercover agents from the ABI to investigate the complaints regular citizens had been sending him letters detailing the activities inside these businesses and town but every time they came back to Montgomery and made the same report. They could not find anything criminal going on in Phenix City, Alabama.

Every law-abiding citizen in town was of the hopes that someone could do something about the criminal activities that he had received so many letters concerning since his election. He had heard the dixie mafia had crime running rampant in their town. He looked for a way to quiet their fears. Everyone was afraid something really bad was going to have to happen before Montgomery would step in and help them. It was not that Montgomery did not want to help them; it was that Montgomery was having trouble getting even their agents to tell them what was going on in the small southern town.

When agents left Montgomery, their commanding officers had given each agent the same orders. They were to investigate reports of criminal activities in this town. With most people and owners of the Clubs in the pocket of the Mafia, none of the agents could find anything or anyone willing to talk about what was going on behind closed doors. No one would help them prove the stories agents inside the State House were hearing. To their disbelief, everyone they sent into the town came back to Montgomery and turned in the same report. Even the agents who did not live-in town were part of "The Machine" before they left to go back to Montgomery. Somehow, "The Machine" managed to get even ABI agents in their pockets by using their various activities inside these houses against them.

When the new agents arrived in Phenix City, the FBI instructed them to go into these establishments as everyday men. Not giving anyone the idea, they were agents of the state looking for proof of the backroom gambling and prostitution that they knew was big in the backwater town. As the agents stayed in town for months at a time, they found Ma and Hoyt had made it easy for them to get caught up in the dealings of these different mafia strongholds. When it was time for them to return to Montgomery, none of the agents showed enough confidence in the information they had collected. None of them felt secure enough that they could provide their bosses sufficient evidence against "The Machine" to shut down the small southern town. None of the agents could get close enough to Ma and Hoyt to find any evidence against those inside the main organization. No one wanted to accept that Hoyt Shepard was the crime boss in Phenix City. He had taken control of the city and the county after his trial for the murder of Lafayette Leebern in 1946.

This time the undercover assignment was planned a little different. A couple of agents had been sent to the governor's office to receive their orders directly from him. Making the governor the only person knowing was being sent to Phenix City. Boy, was the man chosen different. He did not look or talk like an agent and Governor Person's was sure if anybody could get the needed evidence against "The Machine" it was him.

Governor Persons suspected that if the Attorney General had found out what he was doing he would put a stop to it. The Governor did not want to think that the person leaking the information to Phenix City Officials was the Attorney General but this time he was not taking the chance of anyone finding out what he had planned to find the truth. Governor Persons was reluctant to do anything about the crime in Phenix City, he was in last few months of his term, and he did not want to cause waves before Big Jim Folsom took the State back over.

Senior Agents were unsure what it was going to take to get the evidence they needed to bring charges against "The Machine" but they were going to continue to try. Some agents realized it may take a while, but hopefully, sooner rather than later, they would figure out how to get the required evidence. With "The Machine" owning higher-ups in Montgomery, the Russell Betterment Society approached the federal government to get them to help get a handle on the lawlessness in their town. Figuring out what was going on in town would take time. It would take a while to get someone close enough to anyone for them to take the chance and talk. Then agents would need to verify the evidence. Agents wanted a convincing case concerning what was going on in town. Undercover agents had to be sure they could make their case stick before they went into Phenix City and arrested anybody. "The Machine" had proven they had too much power in town to let any agents in without an airtight case against them.

When agents came from Montgomery to the small town most of them found the services reported to them, by the B-girls, being offered outside the Clubs with none of them ever going inside the Club. They allowed these agents to gamble as much as they wanted. While they were gambling agents would speak with others inside the club. Inside the Club, they would find a special woman and go to her room. When agents returned to Montgomery and asked to recount their stories all of them refused. Every agent that had been sent to Phenix City told the same story when their bosses asked. Agents, in charge of the investigation, realized it was going to be hard to prove the activities those first ABI agents reported.

Everyone thought the men they assigned to go to Phenix City were reluctant to testify about what they experienced inside the clubs because they saw nothing. Nothing, to their amazement, could have been further from the truth. When an agent came to town to investigate the businesses, the appeal of the women and the gambling was so strong the lure of the goings-on inside the Clubs was stronger than their ability to control their desires. These men knew they had been sent to Phenix City to do a job but the lure of what they witnessed inside these Clubs was too strong for any of them to resist.

After a while, the Agents Montgomery sent to investigate realized Ma and Hoyt were getting their agents into embarrassing situations, taking pictures, and then keeping the incriminating evidence until they needed it as leverage. When anyone from the State tried to bring cases against the leaders their attorneys used the material "The Machine" gathered to sway the men's testimony. With their extortion material well in hand, Mafia leaders exploited the material to get those facing charges to deny them in court. They had discovered an excellent form of extortion that gave them to use what they had on the agents to keep their mouths shut. If the agents in Montgomery ever realized what had happened inside those houses, they could have their badges taken from them. Agents who had been to Phenix City would deny learning anything even if they worked for the State Troopers Office or the Alabama Bureau of Investigations to protect themselves and their families.

Men from the Attorney General's office expected to find someone from the small town to testify against "The Machine." They needed answers to questions deputies were asking between themselves and others inside the businesses. Answers dealing with the practices in the city especially interested everyone in Montgomery. When the State looked into the reports of criminal activities in Phenix City everybody thought getting the information officials needed could come from employees or regular citizens without a lot of effort. Everyone kept wondering how Ma and Hoyt knew what was going on before the operative ever left Montgomery.

Montgomery officials had sent someone nobody would ever think of being a law enforcement officer. It never occurred to those in Montgomery how close this latest agent would get to just how accurate the reports other agents had given them about Phenix City. When officials revealed who the gentleman was, state agents sent to investigate and gather evidence against "The Machine," everyone would be in total disbelief. He did not look as though he was old enough to have gone through the academy, let alone, take part in an undercover operation like the one he had been assigned to conduct while he was in town.

THAT FIRST LIBERTY

To their astonishment, Brian and Mark found the city a carbon copy of the small town where they grew up. Pine Mountain also had a flare for the dangerous side of life. Harris County as a whole had a reputation for Klan activity on any given Saturday night. When they both applied for ranger training at Fort Benning from their different post. Mark and Brian had not spoken to each other for months and had no idea the other was even thinking of applying.

Military officials in Washington, D.C. had tucked Fort Benning away alongside the banks of the Chattahoochee River. Ranger School became a part of Infantry training in 1951 which brought in a few more recruits during the year for the business owners in Phenix City to exercise their wiles. Being from a small town up the road from Phenix City everyone who came to the town thought they knew what was happening inside the city limits. Rumors of the kinds of things a person could find in town were of no concern to Brian since he, like everyone else, assumed he knew what was actually going on in town.

Everyone believed it, and he had seen other places like Phenix City while growing up and while he traveled before, he joined the military. Brian was well aware of what happened in a town that had those kinds of services and not to be there alone during the early morning hours. Most of the time, he had found, these stories had been exaggerated to get more people to come to see for themselves, but Phenix City was a whole new experience from anything Brian had experienced anywhere in the world.

Brian came to Fort Benning hoping ranger training would help him hone his given mode of service skills. He wanted to find something that allowed him to discover who he was and get away from always doing what his father thought he should do to reach his goals. Brian wanted his time in the military to be his but so far everything Washington, D.C. had approved for him was something or somewhere his father asked them to send Brian.

As soon as he finished breakfast, after he got in his required morning physical training, he planned to wander around the base for a little while to give the old place the once over. He was curious to see if the place even resembled the base, he remembered or had the Department of Defense made so many changes to the base while the military stationed, he and Mark, in other parts of the country that it would be unrecognizable to him. Did they leave anything he remembered from his basic training days two years before? To his surprise, he found the base still looked and felt like the place he had trained during those early days of his military career.

He walked back to the barracks and got ready for the vigorous training he had been promised to begin. Brian hurried outside to join the other trainees for their first morning. They prepared him, he thought, for whatever these next ten weeks could throw at him. Brian and the other candidates were now being asked to remain on the base for the first two weeks. Officials determined that if candidates traveled into town too soon, they would come back broke. Not having enough money to send home to their parents or even buy any of the necessities they would need. They would not have the money to pay anyone for the essentials of everyday living. Nobody got to skip starting their day with physical training. Not even those who occupied those soft comfortable jobs at other duty stations. His training officers thought he was there to get through the training on his family name. Little did anyone realize Brian was tired of being carried because of his family name and wanted to make it through this training on his own merits.

Brian welcomed the challenging work and was ready for whatever the drill sergeant threw at him. He was where he was to make his career in the military that much better. Brian struggled to make it into the first class, but he missed the deadline to get in by one day. He was ready to begin his training. Brian wanted no one to say he got where he was because of his parents' money. It was not his father's money he cared everything about. It was his father he wanted, just once, to make proud. Brian was not the type to sit behind a desk and push a pencil all day. He could not find any duty station that would make anyone proud of his accomplishments, while he worked behind a desk. Brian wanted to be on the front lines, he wanted to see more of the action.

After two long weeks, Brian and the other men would be ready to get their first weekend liberty. They had been closed up on base for the last fourteen days. All the men realized they could use something to take their minds off what they were doing during training. A little relaxation and someone to spend the time with. Drinking, playing pool, and some gambling seemed a much better alternative to sitting on base one more minute.

Brian decided he wanted to go somewhere he could get his blood pumping. He loved the rush he got when he was doing things that were dangerous. Brian would tackle everything that would make him feel as though he could conquer the world. He had heard some of the men talking about a man from Shiloh, Georgia who had the most daring sideline, and Brian wanted to try to track him down. All Brian knew about him was that he was known to build fast cars and take chances driving for whoever would pay him the most money to deliver their illegal whiskey.

During those two weeks of training, Brian overheard Mark and a few of the others talking about the young women at the houses and clubs in Phenix City. What he overheard his fellow trainees talking about dealing with a few of these girls intrigued him. To him, they sounded just like the type of young woman he could see himself having a fun time with. Brian never dreamed any young woman would be able to move him to take her home to Pine Mountain. No one ever tempted him that way, and he could not believe that one lady he heard about could move him in that way, either.

He was, however, intrigued by the conversation these women were causing on base. Most of the men from Fort Benning understood there were two clubs in town that the women in the brothel were out of this world: the Blue Bonnet and Ma Beachies. Brian decided he would try Ma's first. Talk of her club intrigued him the most and he wanted to see what all the fuss was about. Some guys told him that the last time they were at Fort Benning there had been this one young woman that would knock your socks off. He decided he would find out if she was worth all the hype she was getting. None of the men knew there had been new women added to Ma's stable and some were sure to knock anyone is socks off, especially Lacey Burt.

When liberty that first Friday night arrived, Brian was ready to go out for a relaxing night. He knew very well he had to go alone because Mark had gotten himself into a situation with the drill sergeant earlier that afternoon. Mark had gotten himself into trouble and his drill sergeant ordered him to stay on base and wrestle with his self-control issues dealing with his need to talk during platoon hikes. Mark knew it would not be the end of the world and he would get to go next week.

As Brian called a taxi to take him to Phenix City. He was reflecting on everything he had experienced in small southern communities since he had been back. Brian was deep in thought and responded as though he did not notice when the driver pulled into Ma Beachies Swing Time Club. So, the driver twisted around in his seat to let Brian know they had reached their destination. As Brian was staring out of the car, the driver wanted to learn if he read the article about General Patton, and he was claiming he wished to flatten Phenix City with one of his tanks. Patton suspected his troops were being taken advantage of, but Patton could not prove who arranged the murder of his recruit during the last class. It seemed that when trouble arose everyone lost their ability to see and refused to admit where they had been when the murder occurred.

Brian got out of the taxi and strolled into Ma Beachies Swing Time Club. It turned out to be an enormous house. If someone had been just passing on the street it would give them the impression of only having one floor. Ma's sat up against Holland Creek and was a block from Broad Street. Ma's driveway turned onto Tenth Avenue and that ran directly into Thirteenth Street. Brian could tell there was a creek running beside Ma's and wondered why the house sat at such an unconventional angle to the Creek. Most of Ma's guests never thought about or even mentioned the trap doors over the creek that her dealers could drop unruly guests out of the Club.

As he walked through the enormous wooden door. Ma met him at the door. She always met the men as they entered her place. It was Ma's house, and she wanted to know who was with her girls. She wanted no one able to take advantage of the girls in her employ. As he and Ma walked toward the bar to get him a drink, she gave him a glance at the rules of the house she expected him to follow.

Brian listened as Ma told him her main rule, "my girls were not to see the men outside of the house. They were not to fall in love with any of their clients. Whether they came back again was as always up to the gentleman. Any girl a gentleman saw was off-limits," and Ma expected everyone to comply with her wishes, to the letter. NO EXCEPTIONS!!

He assured Ma he understood and would be more than willing to keep himself in check. Brian and Ma talked a few minutes longer and afterward, she walked to get the young woman she had chosen for him. When Ma walked back into the room, she introduced Brian to Lacey Burt. While they sat in the main room, they could see the floor show that was going on in the next room.

Ma being a creature of habit left Lacey with Brian. She retreated to her office to finish some paperwork. Ma had a lot of confidence in Lacey, and she felt she could deal with the rest of the evening. Ma walked into her office and closed the door. Not once did she check to make sure Lacey was doing the job she was hired to perform.

Brian Approaches Ma

When he and Lacey finished that first Friday night, Brian approached Ma Beachies door. He knocked on the door and waited for Ma to come to the door. As Ma opened the door Brian asked if he could have a few minutes of her time to speak with her about another venture he had heard about her being a part of?

"What can I do for you, Brian?"

"I have heard several stories about you and Hoyt Shepard running bootleg whiskey on Friday nights and I would like to apply to be one of those drivers next Friday night."

"Sure thing, here is the application fill it out and hand it to Alex on your way out."

"Yes, ma'am."

"Brian, you are a soldier at Fort Benning, where do you plan on getting a car?"

"I am from Pine Mountain I have several in the garage that I can use for such an undertaking."

"Give Alex a way to contact you this weekend on your way out."

"I will and thank you for this opportunity."

As Brian approached the door, he thought that Alex looked familiar. On his way out he asked,

"Do I know you from somewhere?"

"Where are you from?"

"Pine Mountain, Georgia."

"I have never been there, but my sister and my other siblings live there now."

"Who is your sister?"

"Emmaline Mitchell."

"Is Mark Mitchell your brother?"

"Yes, he is my baby brother."

"He is my best friend."

"Why isn't he with you tonight?"

"He got in trouble for talking during our hike this afternoon and had to stay on base. He will be in here next Friday night."

"Thanks for telling me."

"Are you going to tell him who you are?"

"Not yet, I need to know he will not run to Emmaline and tell her where I am."

As Brian walked out of Ma Beachies he felt as though the world had given him the opportunity to have a little real fun. He got into a cab and told the driver to take him to the

Wilchair Plantation in Pine Mountain. As soon as Brian got the information out of his mouth the driver told him,

"I am not allowed to go there without permission from the family."

"I am Brian Wilchair, I am their son, and I don't need their permission for you to take me home for the weekend."

When Brian arrived, he pressed the buzzer and told the grounds keeper who it was. He immediately opened the gate, and the taxi driver could take him the rest of the way to the house. Brian paid the driver and walked up the steps to the front door, he opened it and went inside. A little after noon Brian went downstairs to see about getting something to eat.

Brian had planned to spend the weekend with his family in Pine Mountain. He preferred to go home and relax in his hammock. He had grown up in the Valley. It thrilled everyone to see him at home, and that he was taking a day to just rest before he had to go back to Columbus and do all that vigorous training all over again. Brian spent the day relaxing, talking to old friends, and experiencing the cuisine of his favorite cook, the family chef.

After dinner he went outside to stare at the stars and try to get the young woman, he had met at Ma's out of his head. No woman before had gotten to him the way she had. Brian fell asleep in the hammock beneath the stars and dreamt of Lacey Burt all night long.

About noon, Alex Mitchell, called Brian to tell him to have him and his car to Ma's as soon as he got Liberty on Friday afternoon. She was allowing him to drive for her next Friday night. He assured Alex that he would be there and that she would not be sorry for giving him this chance.

Brian drove his fastest car back to Fort Benning. Brian would be at Ma's after he got Liberty that Friday afternoon. He was looking forward to it, Brian had not had anything to get his blood pumping in a long time and was looking forward to this chance.

On Friday afternoon, he arrived at Ma's about 5:30 and was there in plenty of time to get his load securely loaded into his car. When he left Ma had given him the instructions of the road to follow, but Brian had been to this destination many times before. He took his own route, and it was a good thing he did. Brian heard on the radio that there was a roadblock on the route that Ma had given him. When he delivered his load an hour early the man asked him how he did that nobody on their first run has ever gotten their load to us early or on time. They have always had trouble with the law somewhere.

"Just lucky I guess."

On the way back to Phenix City, Brian thought about the promise he had made Ma. He would not see Lacey outside Ma Beachies Swing Time Club. Brian knew, he wanted to see more of her after that night. He found he could not get Lacey out his thoughts. No woman, a lady of the evening, had ever touched him the way she did. Brian could tell she was different which caused him to want to see her even more.

During liberty, the next week Brian waited for Lacey to leave Ma's. While she walked home, Brian walked up beside her.

"Can I escort you home?"

"Ma and her managers do not want us to get involved with clients outside of work."

"I know but I cannot help myself."

"If we get caught one or both of us could get hurt."

"I will take the chance if you take a chance to see me."

"I would like that very much, Brian."

Brian walked Lacey home that night. He gave no thought to what might happen to them if they got caught with each other. Brian, at this point, did not care what happened to him. Lacey Kasey Burt intrigued him, and he wanted to find out what it was about her that caused her to be so special from the other girls he had dated.

As Brian and Lacey neared the driveway of the house Lacey said was hers. She and Brian planned to meet each other at the waterfall on Summerville Road the next afternoon. Brian looked at his watch it was after two in the morning, and nobody was out that time of night. He walked back to the corner of her street, stood there, and observed her as she walked into her home.

Brian spun around and walked back, taking his time, to arrive at his car. He had no idea if Lacey was going to keep their date, or if she was going to stand him up. Brian had every intention of being where he had requested her to meet him, come hell or high water.

Brian left Pine Mountain in enough time to get to Phenix City and keep his date with Lacey. He arrived first. Brian had brought with him a picnic basket packed with Chicken, mashed potatoes, grapes, wine, a small block of cheese, and bread. While he waited for Lacey, he arranged the cloth on the ground and arranged the food while he waited. He so hoped she did not stand him up. After what seemed to be an eternity, Lacey walked up to where he was relaxing on the ground.

Lacey was wearing a pair of blue jeans and a nice top. She looked like she was more at ease with him on that grassy knoll than she had been that first night. Lacey was a little apprehensive and aloof when it came to individuals she did not know very well. She walked over to Brian and sat down beside him.

Brian handed her a frosty glass of tea that he had poured out of a bottle his mom had discovered on a trip to Egypt. Both of them thought it would be appropriate for Brian to use the bottle when he wanted to pack water or tea in his locker. Even though he was aware, he could not keep that kind of stuff in his footlocker he did not argue with his mom.

He and Lacey sat there on the blanket for hours talking and getting to know each other. Brian found out they had forced Lacey into taking a job with Ma. She could not find employment anywhere else, and her parents had told her she had a brief time to find a job. Lacey had no idea what else to do. She needed the money but no one, except Ma, would give her the opportunity to prove to them, what she could do.

As they sat there talking, they flirted with one another. Brian was reluctant to take it too quick. He was wondering if he would scare her off if he went too fast. Brian wanted her to tell him everything about herself. They sat there that afternoon talking about everything. Lacey explained to him how she felt about being an employee at Ma's. He looked at her and let her know he understood her concerns.

"Why do you do the job?"

"Because it is the only one, I can find in this area."

"You dislike your job?"

"No, I detest it, but it is all I could find to try to get out of my parents' home."

Brian and Lacey sat there and talked for hours. They made plans for next Sunday afternoon. He told her he did not expect he would be into Ma's during the next week his father had something he wanted him to do. They did not wish the afternoon to come to an end, but they both knew they had to return to the real world. Brian had to be back on the base in a little while. He did not need to give anyone a reason to show him as AWOL and have anyone ask questions. Brian knew all too well what it meant that the two of them were sitting there together. He had met her at Ma's and acknowledged the rules before she introduced him to Lacey during his first Friday night visit.

Brian and Lacey walked to their cars and shouted they would see each other in a week. He could not wait until Sunday. Lacey infatuated him with her blonde hair, blue eyes, and long legs. Coming from the place they me that first night, Lacey was nothing like he thought. Brian would make the most of the week, but to him, the week crept by. Before the week concluded, he had remarked to Mark several times that "this one week seems like all ten thrown together." He thought many times during the week that it was dragging on. It was hard for him to tell if the week had just progressed that slowly or if Brian was just excited about what he had planned for Sunday afternoon.

Mark Mitchell

Ranger Training was new to the United States Army. Mark had wanted to be a part of that initial class, but he missed being in that first class by two days. His commanding officer could not carry out the preparations for him to travel back to Georgia to attend the training with the duties he had to complete in Kansas coming first.

Mark thought his chance had passed him by. He was not aware this was a unique course army officials planned to present once a year. They would seek only the best and brightest to take the course, and this course would break even some of them. They might assume they were tough, but they created this course to locate the weaknesses everyone seemed to have. To get through and be a Ranger an individual would have to be a special type of man to tolerate what the program would throw at them. Army officials did not allow women to apply to Ranger Training in those beginning years of the program.

While he waited for the next class to begin, he received some necessary training to keep his skills up to date. That afternoon when his commanding officer approached him about the new class for Ranger Training that was to begin in March. Over the moon with emotion by being approached with a request to go through Ranger training with the second class.

Mark accepted the invitation before anybody could have the chance to change their minds. When he got back to the barracks that evening, he called Brian to tell him the news. While they were talking Brian, told him the news of his being asked to attend as well.

Both men felt a lot of joy to be going back to Fort Benning and for them to be together again. They had not seen each other since Army representatives had deployed them after basic training. Before basic training, they had been inseparable.

After they checked in at Fort Benning and the week began all during the week being nervous about their unknown training. To them, it was like being back in high school, Brian and Mark staying up late doing their homework before lights out those first two weeks. Brian was good with anything that dealt with Math and Mark was good at all the other stuff they threw at them. These two complimented the other so much a person from the outside could tell they were best of friends they were with each other.

On Thursday afternoon of that second week, the men ran for a five-mile with the gear they required for the field on his backs. Mark had become tired and spoke to the other men in the ranks. He had everybody laughing before they finished their run.

Drill Sergeants did not like the things taking place within the company that would cause everyone to laugh and cut up, so they added more distance to the hike; for everybody. As they were running back to the base Mark learned, he would not be getting liberty that Friday night, he would stay behind to clean toilets and perform their morning exercises. Marks weekend would be at the sympathy of the Drill Sergeant to determine what he thought was fit retribution for his conduct during the hike.

Mark got up the next morning when the bugler played revile. Each morning a representative of the army's band got up and played notifying everyone to get out of bed and start the day. As he made his way to the mess hall to get something to eat, he could not help but wish he were with Brian during their first liberty.

After breakfast, Mark met his Drill Sergeant in front of the barracks. He told Mark they would have two days of fun. Mark would spend the rest of his Saturday doing push-ups and jumping jacks. When he tired of watching Mark, do these exercises the Drill Sergeant ran around in circles while raising his rifle over his head. He kept doing his exercises the whole time the Drill Sergeant was spraying Mark with icy water.

When they concluded with the water torture that afternoon Mark and his Drill Sergeant went inside to take a shower. After showering Mark was to report to the mess hall to get something to eat and be back in the barracks before 7:00 p.m. He was not to leave his barracks after 7:00 p.m. until the next morning.

Mark finished Sunday with his toothbrush in his hand. He was to clean the latrine with it and the stairs going into the barracks. If the Drill Sergeant found one particle of dirt, he would have to do it until he got all the dirt and grime off the floor. They wanted the floors shiny where you could serve food off the floors.

As he wrapped up with the last of the stairs and was putting everything away, the others came back from their weekend in town. Mark was standing at the top of the stairs waiting for Brian when he came back. He was curious about how his best friends' weekend had gone. Mark completed his long weekend. His commanding officer had given him until Monday morning to determine if Ranger The training was for him or if he wanted to go back to Leavenworth to finish out his tour of duty.

Mark came down for chow that Monday morning with a what seemed to everyone as a fresh lease on life and on his place in the group. He acted more like a collaborator and a leader than an individual who had no ambition and all he wanted out of life was to be the class comedian.

As he came into the dining hall, he noticed his Drill Instructor sitting there and strolled over to him. His Drill Sergeant told him during the weekend to figure out why he wanted to remain in the program. Given a once in a lifetime opportunity, Mark realized he was one of the lucky ones and had no intention of throwing that good luck in the trash can and going back without completing what he had started, he had come too far to throw it all away now.

JUNE BENNING

June Benning was the daughter, of the grandson, of Civil War hero Fort Benning had been named to honor. Named after Henry L. Benning, a brigadier general in the Confederate States Army during the Civil War. Since 1909, Fort Benning has served as the Home of the Infantry. She also had the honor of being Lacey's best friend since they were small children. June and Lacey had grown up next door to each other, and as kids were inseparable. According to those in the neighborhood talking to June was easy.

Most everyone who knew her found they could tell her anything, but in the last few weeks, Lacey found she could not talk to June, or anyone else, about the horrors she had seen during her first two weeks of work. She did not think her friend could handle what she was having to do to make a living. Lacey did not want June judging her because of the type of work she had to take. June, a tall, skinny, brown-haired, and brown-eyed young lady. Nothing special to look at, but she had her share of gentleman callers. June was a sensible and fun-loving young girl who would be a delightful addition to Ma's stable. She had a style when it came to lighting up a room because of her cheerful smile and temperament. If someone were down, she would try to make their day just a little brighter.

June waited that Saturday night until Lacey came home from Ma's. She needed to see if Lacey would be willing to recommend her for a position at Ma Beachies. June was getting cabin fever, and there were not a lot of jobs in the local area. Unless you wanted to go to work for one of the local mills, there was nothing interesting going on in town to keep a girl entertained.

One of June's other friends told her what went on at Ma Beachies Swing Time Club. She pointed out that the cash she could make during a week was well worth the emotional toll it took on some young women. June could see nothing inappropriate about what her friend was telling her and assumed she would be allowed to meet many distinct kinds of men during her career. There was nothing in town paying that kind of wage that was respectable, so a little excitement made it even more enticing.

That Sunday, Lacey told Ma Beachies about June. Ma expressed an interest and wanted her to come in and meet with her about working during the week. June was impatient to meet Lacey's employer, and June had wanted to join Ma's stable of young women for a while. During the next week, she would go down to talk to Ma Beachies about becoming part of her stable.

June understood all too well what kind of place Ma Beachies ran. She had no doubts about beginning the work. June felt she could keep her home life and her work life separate. She was all too ready to sacrifice to make the kind of money she was aware traveled through Ma Beachies on any given night. Even someday she could work her way up to Friday and Saturday nights. She heard from some of the other girls she knew who worked for Ma that was where the true money could be made. To the right young lady, being able to handle the duties, put upon a woman Ma's could be an easy job.

Ma gave her the position that Monday afternoon. June accepted the offer with no issues about what the job entailed. They instructed June to report to the house a little before six o'clock that afternoon. Someone willing to give her the opportunity to get a job delighted June. She could not deal with her emotions any longer. Even knowing what kind of work, Ma Beachies engaged in did not matter to her; she looked forward to making her clients have an enjoyable time and feel good about themselves.

Ma Beachies

Soldiers from Fort Benning, soon-to-be warriors, would make a special trip to watch the floor show, to make passes at the B-girls, to drink, to gamble, to let one dancer test the bedsprings, and then to fight if the girl that caught their attention looked at someone else. Even students from nearby Alabama Polytechnic Institute, today known as Auburn University, flocked to "Ma's" as a favorite hangout on Friday and Saturday night. Of all the nightclubs, honky-tonks, cafes, casinos, snuggeries, haunts, retreats, roosts, shacks, shanties, hutches, cowsheds, huts, lodges, courts, alehouses, gin mills, bars, saloons, speakeasies, hovels, kennels, booths, and stalls in Phenix City, none could compare with "Ma's" for the soldier-student clientele. Ma's was proving to be the place to be for men of any age on any given Friday or Saturday night. If a man wanted a certain kind of entertainment, he would find it in Phenix City all he had to do was go looking for a fun time. It was on every corner downtown, there was no getting around all the houses. They were lined up next to the river on all roads leading into the town.

Ma's sister would try to give her some competition by building her business right down the road. When Ma was having a good night and capacity was over the limit, they would send the overflow down the road. Ada Eberhart, owner of the Lasso

Club, liked to get her thrills from a vial and a bottle. She was a gruff woman and a woman who attracted a seeder kind of clientele. These two women may have been sisters, but they had personalities that gave their clubs much different atmospheres. Ada's Place looked like a haunted house sitting in wait for the unexpecting young man.

Ma's Swing Club was built along Thirteenth Street and alongside Holland Creek and the Chattahoochee River. Nestled back off of the road down what looked like from the road a dirt path. Ma always kept five or six exceptional girls working on any given weekday night. She saved her best girls for the soldiers and locals who came in on Friday and Saturday nights so she would be sure to make more money on those nights. Ma was aware if she kept the best for the weekends, you would not lose as much money by being closed on Sundays. With no one in town wanting to believe that organized crime had moved into their small town all the business owners agreed to keep up a certain kind of facade around town.

According to Ma, these men, who came in on Friday and Saturday nights, were the big tippers and deserved the girls who would give them that special touch they had been craving all week. Sundays, however, were always a day of rest for everyone. These club owners had to keep up the appearances of running a law-abiding establishment. No one wanted to know they had mafia living in their small, quiet town.

She did have some shady looking characters working for her. Ma controlled most of the town's law enforcement. She gathered by whatever means necessary enough information on the dealings of the sheriff and Police Chief to guarantee their loyalty. Ma and Hoyt made sure those on their payroll could do business as they pleased. Ma was a woman to avoid and most of the town knew it. If Ma told someone to do something, she meant for someone to carry it out. Things Ma and other business owners asked employees to do were to happen the way she told them, and no one argued with her. Not even the man who owned the town and brought in the kinds of games that brought the business inside the city limits would dare say too much to this small stature woman.

Ma ran the local gambling house she tucked away beside Holland Creek. Government officials from Montgomery tried to conduct surprise raids on Ma's Swing Time Club twice in recent memory, but her control reached to the State Capitol in Montgomery. To her credit, she used the officials she extorted to get them to do what she wanted. She told both the sheriff and the chief of police if it would not hurt her business; she was fine with everyone doing their job the proper way to keep the community safe. But if it would cost her anything, she wanted whatever someone was planning squashed before it could get out of hand. Ma was aware her business was of great concern in Montgomery. There was, however, someone on her payroll with more pull than any of the others she had extorted before. He was her way of keeping her business dealings away from law enforcement who wanted to shut her down and put her in jail.

Most of the town was sure of who she was and what her establishment was all about if you were male and looking for a suitable time. But one summer night, someone contacted the authorities outside of the small southern town. Marshal's and police raided Ma's place looking for the illegal operation one of the concerned citizens of Phenix City had told them about. All they found when they walked into the place was a nice night club with alcohol, singing, and patrons playing pool in the back of the bar. Nothing nefarious here, she heard from the informant they placed in Montgomery, he would call Ma and warn her a raid was about the happen. This gave management time to hide other parts of her establishment before the authorities could get to her place.

No one in Montgomery knew how word got to Ma so fast to clean her act up, but with as many people on her payroll as she was lucky enough to have gathered over the years. Someone would be good enough to tip her off before they could carry out their raid. When the raid was to happen, the person hidden in Montgomery agreed to call, as a part of their responsibilities, to let them know they would come to town to raid the gambling house. For a while, every time they got word of a raid, they would call Ma and let her know well in advance who and what was coming her way.

Ma hired June on the spot. She put her to work for the time being during the week. Ma wanted to see what June could do. If Ma's gut feeling about her was right June would be one of the weekend girls in no time. Ma had a sixth sense about these kinds of things, which is why she made such a good living as the owner of the Swing Time Club.

Brian came in a little early that Friday afternoon. He wanted to see Lacey, but she was not due to come to work for another hour. Brian had other plans that evening and wanted to relax a little bit before he made that long trip to Pine Mountain. He wanted to work off some of the tension that had followed him from Fort Benning that afternoon. June was there until the weekend girls arrived. Brian agreed to see her that afternoon, but when they reached her room, Brain began to have second thoughts about having anything to do with her. He thought she was a pretty girl, but something about her he did not like. She was no Lacey and he wanted to keep himself for her. When they reached her room, he turned to her and told her he was sorry, but he could not go through with what he had come in for.

When Brian rejected her, she seemed to go off the deep end. She began asking him if he thought she was not good enough for him? Brian looked as though someone had slapped his face, he could not believe she was having a problem with him changing his mind. As he walked out of her door, he laid her money on her nightstand and walked down the stairs and out of the house into the bright sunlight. All he could make out as he walked to his car was the Cicada as they sang in the trees around Holland Creek.

As he walked to his car, he understood June to yell to him he would regret walking out on her. She was as good as Lacey, better. The last words he heard her say was,

"I will get even with you for this, watch your back."

As she finished her rant at him, he got into his car and drove toward the 14th Street Bridge. He was going to Pine Mountain to begin his weekend earlier than he had planned. Brian did not give the events of that afternoon another thought. To him it was not worth his time to worry about every girl, woman, he had ever made mad by walking out on them when he had gotten them all worked up.

*****

Most weeks when there was no one around, people who could identify any of the parties involved from outside the city, political leaders from Montgomery would come down and meet with Ma and Hoyt. These busy men would often include some other business owners in their meetings but there could be no witnesses to their dealings. When these meetings took place bouncers would make sure no one they did not know got anywhere near the business where these meetings were being held. Whoever, they allowed to be at these meetings had to have tight lips and would let nothing anyone said to make its way to anyone else's ears. Ma always had three of her bodyguards with her at all times, Alex, Andy, and Kent.

During a normal week when one of these officials came to town it was Silas Garrett, the Attorney General for the State of Alabama. Nowhere did he go that he did not have a bodyguard with him. Everyone knew when he came to town, he had to have someone watch his back. Everyone in town wanted to get rid of him. He could not get things passed in the State House fast enough. They had found out he had to operate by some written laws of the state. He had just got around most of them so "The Machine" could continue to carry on their illegal activities.

When Silas came to town, he would ask to see one of the girls. For the last couple of months, he had been seeing June and she was the only one he wanted to see. He liked the way she made him feel and he was getting the impression he could talk to her about anything. Si liked women even though he married his wife years ago. He still liked to visit the women in Phenix City. But June was different, and everyone knew it, at least, in Silas Garrett's heart.

LACEY'S PERCEPTION

When Lacey accepted work from Ma that summer morning, she told herself she would work this job for two months. It had already been four with no end in sight. Lacey did not like the way her work made her feel about herself or her life. She would have loved to find a nice nine to five secretarial job and live at home with her parents, at this point. Lacey was considering taking some business courses at the local college during the week, but so far, she could not bring herself to quit her position with Ma. Only the thought of how good the money was from those two nights kept her going back each week. Lacey made enough money on Friday and Saturday night; she did not have to work another job during the week. She had the week to do whatever she wanted with her time and spend it with whoever she wished.

Lacey met a bunch of men on the Friday and Saturday nights she worked. Most of them just made her feel sleazy about herself. They set her up that Friday night with the Mayor of Phenix City. They informed her to show him the time of his life. Lacey was also told he was a big tipper, and she was to be extra nice to him.

She met the mayor as he came in. Took him to her suite for a chance to get to recognize him a little before, she would try to show him an enjoyable time. For some reason, the man just made her skin crawl. To her, he was the absolute definition of scum, but she did not get compensated for her opinion. While she was talking with him, he requested that she give him a blow job before they had sex.

Lacey walked over to where he was sitting, lifted her leg and draped it around his waist. She slid herself down onto his lap; unfortunately, she caught sight of herself in the mirror. Lacey could not accept it was her image she saw being reflected in the mirror back at her. Where had the girl she was just four months before gone? Repulsed by what she saw, she never let it show in the attention she devoted to her clients during any night.

She longed for the days when her parents took care of her. Lacey wanted to be that sheltered little girl again. Nowhere could she find anyone who would hide her from herself and what she was feeling towards herself. What would her mother think if she could witness what she made her into in just four brief months? Lacey was unsure she would ever look at herself in the mirror the same way again. Her self-respect was getting lower by the day, and she was looking for a way to leave Mas and continue to make the same money she had become accustomed to at the Swing Club.

Lacey unbuttoned and unzipped the mayor's slacks and slid them down out of her way. She lowered herself onto him, feeling him penetrate her as she slid down on him. Repulsed by what she was doing but could find no way out. She continued what they employed her to do. As she continued to show him the special attention, supervisors told her to offer him, she kissed the corner of his mouth, taunting him with her tongue. Giving him just enough to make him react and crave more of her. After a little while, he picked her up, strolled over to the bed with her in his arms. Laying her on the bed he had sex with her. When he finished with her, he let out a hoot they heard in the next chamber.

After he finished with her, he left her money on the bedside stand. He walked downstairs to the gambling room continuing his night of satisfaction. Lacey lay on her bed for a few minutes struggling to forget what had just taken place. She wanted nothing more than to run home and never go back, but that management told her was a sure-fire way to get her executed.

Lacey dreaded getting up off the bed but after a while she did. She got dressed and strolled downstairs to the gambling room like she had so many times before. She sat down beside him and observed as he played one bad hand after another. Lacey was doing nothing for his luck that night. He lost massive sums of money every time they dealt the cards to him. After a while, he asked her if she minded getting him a drink. She was overjoyed to do anything to get away from him and the way he made her feel about herself.

After getting the mayor his drink, she walked back up to her room. She was no longer needed in the gambling room and could get another client in before midnight. Lacey felt empty and dirty when Brian came sauntering into her room. She did not feel up to any more men that evening, but she knew she had a job to do and expected to make everyone's dreams come true.

As she turned around, she realized she had seen the young man before. Lacey remembered him from the weekend before they had spent together. They sat beside the fire talking about how their respective weeks had gone. Lacey wanted nothing more than to hole up there in her room. She did not feel she could be a satisfactory date for anyone that night.

Lacey noticed that every time she looked into Brian's eyes; she had this sudden rush of nausea in her stomach. She could feel her cheeks flushing and hoped he could not see what was taking place with her. Lacey became hot, she could not figure out what was going on for a few seconds before she saw herself in the mirror and felt cold and ugly. She experienced, that night, one of the worst nights of her life.

"Brian, do you mind just holding me for a little while tonight?"

"No, it would delight me to stay and hold you, if that is what you want. Can I ask what happened that has you feeling so bad about yourself?"

"I had to make love to a man tonight that made me feel even dirtier than I do every other night when I leave here to go home."

"Come over here. All we have to do tonight is talk. That is enough for me. I enjoy your company. If talking is all you wish to do tonight that is what we will do."

Brian and Lacey sat on the bed for a long time. As they sat there, in her room, she wanted Brian to caress her, but she did not wish to remember him the way she remembered most of the men she saw. Brian kissed the corner of her mouth. He told her if she wanted to quit just say so and he would. That night all she wanted was to feel better about herself. Someone to make her remember what was good about love and living.

As Brian kissed her lips, she could feel a burning sensation all over her body. He made her feel in a way she had never felt before. Lacey smiled at Brian and his heart softened into a heap of soft mush. Lacey took the pillows off her bed and spread them on the floor in front of the fireplace. She sat down softly and patted the floor beside her. Lacey wanted Brian as close to her as she could get him. She wrapped her arms around his waist. Kissed him with her whole being. Ran her hand over his chest and unbuttoned his shirt and slipping her arms under Brian's t-shirt. Lacey raised Brian's arms and slid both shirts off at the same time.

Reaching down she unzipped his blue jeans and slid them down enough so she could see his military skivvies. She reached her hand inside his underwear and caressed his aroused parts. Lacey knew by his reaction she was getting to him. He wanted her as much as she wanted him. They were taunting each other with their playfulness and tongue play.

Lacey slid around in front of Brian and hoisted herself onto him. As he was making love to her, she felt herself melt into his arms. She felt protected in Brian's arms and wanted him to want her as much as she wanted him. She could feel him satisfying parts of her that no man she had been with since she came to Ma Beachies had reached. To her, this incident was something she never encountered from any of the men she met at Ma Beachies.

She was not paying attention when he picked her up to lay her on the floor, her head leaning on a pillow. Engrossed in what she was feeling, Lacey liked the way her body tingled with every touch of his body to hers. She still moved as his body moved, but now he was in control. Lacey gave into the tempo he set for the two of them. Slow and deliberate, she seemed in paradise. She had found paradise in Brian's embrace. She knew she had felt nothing like that before. Lacey did not want him to finish with her; she wanted more. She whispered to him, "not yet." Brian realized what she wanted and went with her again. Deliberate, gentle affecting every part of her body and being wanted more, and he was fulfilling her like no one else ever had.

When they finished both let out a soft moan of surrender that seemed to come from their souls, it was so gentle. Lacey and Brian sunk into each other. They held each other for a few minutes struggling to figure out what had just taken place in her room. Brian got up off the floor where he had just made love to this gorgeous woman. He wanted nothing more than to stay with her, but he knew his time with her was up.

Before he left, he left her money on the stand. That night he did not go to the gambling room because he did not think he could concentrate on cards. He was too busy thinking about Lacey, the way she made every fiber of his being feel. Brian had known no other woman who could make him feel like this.

He was experiencing feelings for this woman, a prostitute that he had never felt for anyone before. Brian knew he was breaking the rules by getting involved with her outside of Mas, but he could not help it. She was all he could think about the rest of the weekend and all the next week. Thoughts of her affected his performance during his training and he could not have that. He knew he had to put her out of his thoughts until he finished his Ranger training. His training was important for this time in his life. He knew it would not thrill his parents if he failed Ranger Training after coming this far. In the back of his mind, he could hear his father saying, "the girl is not worth your time. Find someone worthy of you." All he wanted was Lacey Burt and there was no way of changing his heart now.

GOVERNOR OF ALABAMA

Seth Gordon Persons became the 42nd Governor of the State of Alabama by running on a platform of reform for the state. Late in his administration and just before the gubernatorial election for his second term the Supreme Court handed down its opinion for the case of Brown vs. Board of Education of Topeka, Kansas. In this decision the nine justices outlawed segregated facilities in public schools. Persons was a moderate on racial issues. He ran for governor on a promise to limit or revoke the poll tax which kept poor whites and Black people from voting. Most residents in the small city could not tolerate Black people and whites using the same water fountain and could not fathom the thought of using the same restrooms. You could forget about whites sending their children to the same school as a Black child. They were so stuck in their ways none of them could see any alternative plan of achieving the things Persons had promised when he became governor.

Violence in the small central Alabama town in the last few months made the Governor realize the city was experiencing violent crimes he and his advisors saw as the final straw. As the news of the murder of Albert Patterson reached Governor Persons' desk, he knew he had to do something, and he had to move fast to keep more of the violence out of the city. Details of the murder of Patterson were given to Person's in detail. It was reported to him, Patterson had been shot in the face as he left his office downtown Phenix City one warm June evening.

Governor Person's placed Russell County under martial law until someone could figure out how to clean up downtown and protect the locals who called the small-town home. As a matter of desperation, nothing else he had tried in the small town had worked, he dispatched the states National Guard troops to defend ordinary citizens from the criminals who owned the city and the officials "The Machine" had put into offices of authority. With national guard troops taking over the town there was a sense that real change was coming. National Guard troops were pulling slot machines, roulette wheels, and blackjack tables out of the back of all the businesses in the downtown area and throwing them all into a big pile outside the jail. When they had them all outside, they set fire to them, and guardsmen sat and watched them as they burned.

Governor Persons briefed State Trooper officers with the information members of the Russell Betterment Association, RBA, had provided his office, the Alabama Bureau of Investigation, ABI, and the State Investigator's office concerning the numerous business and citizen complaints. Their information detailed what was taking place in two-night clubs in downtown Phenix City and some of the other activities they suspected. No one had gotten anyone to talk about what was going on inside the Clubs operating in the small town. Some agents had reported enough back to Montgomery that their bosses could prove some of the accusations residents had made, but no one could use their reports to make the charges stick. Everyone was tight-lipped about what they had witnessed inside those businesses. When an agent left to go back to Montgomery, they had committed enough crimes they feared for their lives if they talked about what they knew. In those days, it was better to keep your mouth shut and listen than it was to talk bino and get your fifteen minutes of fame. No one wanted to be the person in the Columbus Ledger-Enquirer in the morning letting the world see your death announcement. So, to everyone's' benefit you kept your mouth shut about what you had found. On the other hand, if you knew nothing you did not speculate about what you thought might be going on downtown. It was none of your business, it was better to leave it that way. If you did not want to wear cement boots and wind up taking a swim with the fish in the Chattahoochee River, you had better keep your mouth shut and pretend you were never there.

In previous visits, the Russell Betterment Association had shown the Governor pictures of Hugh Bentley's home where someone had put dynamite under the front of his house and blown that portion of his house up. It was a tough time to be living in Phenix City. Some in town saw their town could benefit from organized crime going away and making the city into a wonderful place to live. The Russell Betterment Association faced the challenge of finding someone who would help them. On occasion it looked like Governor Persons was going to turn them away like other Governors before him. It surprised Bentley when on his second visit to the capitol Person's agreed to help the RBA find a solution to the corruption in Phenix City and clean the city up. Persons reply to Bentley's statement, "Someone may have to get killed before anyone in the Alabama government helps us." Governor Persons could not believe his ears that someone thought he was that uncaring. Bentley's statement made cold shivers run up Person's spine at the implications of such a statement.

When agents returned to their offices in Montgomery and gave the same report which were given to familiarize themselves with the people and the clubs in the area. Reports read the same as the ones they were given when they were assigned to investigate Phenix City corruption. These reports read as though someone was dictating what they were to say when they returned to Montgomery. Agents who were given the assignment to go to the small town were reluctant to swear to the validity of the reports. None of the agents had any desire to talk to their bosses or anyone else about what happened to them while they were in Phenix City, but everyone had an idea what was happening while they were away from the watchful eyes of those in charge. Agents did not want to talk for fear of their families being torn apart or even worse, being killed while away from home. Agents got the proof the governor needed to clean up the town, but they let themselves get caught in compromising positions inside the Swing Club or the Blue Bonnet. When that happened Ma and Hoyt both could find a way to get the men into compromising positions that would cause the agents considerable damage to their personal reputations or even worse "The Machine" could kill them. Before they left town, they were told that if they did not keep their mouths shut their families' lives and their own would be in danger. These men had friends in high places, and they were not afraid to use them.

While they waited for the men from Montgomery to arrive for their visit, Ma and Hoyt would cover up the normal business of the house. It would not take them long; they could hide their tracks before anyone could make it eighty miles from Montgomery. They left the State House with no option but to admit there might be someone inside the Office of the Governor on the payroll of "The Machine" in Phenix City. Someone who would tell them when and who was being dispatched to investigate the accusations. Not this time, though, Persons had other ideas. He was sending two groups of investigators, one who came from the normal ABI and Investigation offices. The other was someone nobody in the statehouse or the city would ever suspect of being an undercover investigator for the governor's office.

After a while, Governor Persons would speak with every new agent several times before sending them on assignment to Phenix City. He wanted to warn them what could happen when they were in these establishments or an establishment of the like in other areas. As Governor he warned his agents about the questionable dealings of these two business owners. Persons had gotten word that Ma and Hoyt knew, somehow, every time he sent an agent before they ever left Montgomery. He sat down with the agents again and again to remind them not to get snagged in their web of lies, they would use their actions against them, and as a result his office would have to start their investigation all over again. It was baffling though how someone in such a small town could have connections all the way to the state capitol. No one ever suspected that the person being paid off was the person in charge of the ABI and the state investigators, Si Garrett. Attorney General Si Garrett was in a position which gave him access to the governors wishes minutes after he made the assignments. When the mafia came in, they bought Garrett with campaign contributions. Now "The Machine" owned him and was obligated to help them anyway his office could.

Citizens gave agents statements that showed there were bordellos and gambling houses which were being run in the middle of downtown. Law enforcement officers taking half the profits from these dens of inequity and then looking the other way when it came to the dealings from the inside their walls. Every time law enforcement assigned a different agent to investigate citizens claims nothing ever came of the investigation. None of the officers or agents could get close enough to the suspected houses of ill-repute without being spotted as law enforcement. They required more time to bring the activities of these businesses to light. Citizens and the RBA were determined to rid their town of the corruption that had taken over no matter what it took. They were determined to leave their children a town to live in that was better than the one they grew up in. Residents and the members of the local churches knew it was possible and one day they would see a town they could be proud of.

To control the agents no matter what happened while they stayed in town Mafia bosses told employees of the various nightclubs and gambling clubs to get everyone into situations which could leave the men facing to charges of their own. No one told officers to get themselves into positions they would be too embarrassed to disclose to anyone. Positions they would never wish their wives to hear about when they went to court to testify against those in Phenix City. It was a well-known fact that officers from the state could use any means that did not break the law to get the evidence needed on anyone. This time, though, to get the evidence on Ma and Hoyt agents needed to break laws passed by the state legislature. None of them knew if they would get into trouble if the state uncovered what they had to do to get the evidence federal agents needed to file charges against those in Phenix City. None of the agents, the governor sent to Phenix City, found they had enough courage to ask if their immunity from prosecution covered positions, they had to put themselves into while they were investigating corruption in this small town. Agents had to pay prostitutes for their services just to see what they would get for their money. Boy had they gotten an education when these ladies finished with them. A job they loved but none of them wanted anyone to realize what kind of levels they had to sink to get their job done. Wives and bosses alike might look at them a little differently in the morning if they ever found out what they did while away from their families.

Montgomery assigned another undercover agent earlier in the day. No one had any idea this time who or when the Governor was going to send the new agent. This time the Governor sent someone to Phenix City to investigate the reports telling no one his exact plan. The Governor told everybody he selected someone to investigate the details his office received about the goings-on inside the city's government and the businesses downtown. Nobody in the State government but the Governor knew who he sent to town and when they would be there to try to catch the clubs in an embarrassing position. This time he wanted no one able to mess up his plan. When the person he sent to town got there, no one would suspect he was in any way associated with the Governor's office, he could pass as a soldier or even a person off the street. He was new to the force and his handling of prior assignments had been without reproach. He .had a reputation of coming back with the results which were needed to solve cases.

As an agent he had proven himself to be quite an asset to the department.

Governor Persons decided no one except himself would have any idea who was going to Phenix City, how they would get there, or when. When the Governor found out who the informer was Hoyt and Ma had paid off inside the Capitol building, he would not know how close they had gotten to him. Their informant would get paid for giving them the date and time in enough time for them to cover up the operations the Governor and his staff were looking for, or so they were all going to be led to believe.

Ma and Hoyt told the managers and the young women that it was business as expected until Friday night two weeks from that day. On that night, Ma expected Lacey to be at work about 6:00 p.m. just like she had done since the day she was hired. The entire change for that week would be she would put on a nice dress and seat people as they showed up for supper. Dinner was something they did not provide often to the public. They extended that privilege only to those who requested the dining room.

Their normal activities for the weeks when Montgomery was to send agents to Phenix City was to just serve dinner. Then after the raid, they would open the gambling hall but not more than was necessary to keep the patrons happy. They relaxed on these Friday nights, and they did not have to justify themselves to the usual crowd who came to Ma Beachies and the Blue Bonnet.

They would clean their businesses up starting a week after the Attorney General advised them, they were planning a raid. Confident she could cover up their activities once again. Ma had worked it out so many times before, she would get the feeling Montgomery was planning something. To their dismay this time was different, she knew it was coming, but to her dismay she could not figure out what, how many, or even when. All of her connections were telling her the same thing. They had no way of finding out what was being organized for this raid. Ma had a sick feeling deep within her stomach this time was going to be different. What concerned her was the informant they had in the inner workings of the administration was of no use because according to them the Governor was keeping his thoughts to himself. Someone who had not been, up until now, part of the Montgomery scene but looked and could pass as a soldier from Fort Benning. That is what the Governor was looking for. He hoped his latest plan worked. It was the best plan he had come up with so far, and if this did not work, he did not know what he was going to try next. Governor Persons was out of ideas and his patience was wearing thin.

BRIAN'S RANGER TRAINING

As soon as Ranger training was over Brian decided he was going to see more of Lacey Burt. He knew what he wanted from her, but he had agreed to follow the rules of Ma Beachies place. Rules which forbid her to see him, but he wanted to see her more. Brian did not care if there were consequences associated with what he wanted. As Ma had told him that first night the consequences of seeing one of her girls other than at the Swing Club could be hard to live with. His experiences bound him and made him even more determined to see this girl who made him feel with every fiber of his being. Brian and Lacey had been seeing each other away from Ma's for the last two weeks. They would find weekends when Brian did not want to come to the house and would go for picnics or to the movies on Sunday afternoons. To try to keep anyone from figuring out that they were seeing each other outside of the Club Brian would come in on Friday night to see Lacey and to do a little gambling. Never anything big just enough to keep down suspicions of those in charge.

He told Mark during the week that he was seeing Lacey and walked her home after she had got off at Ma's. Mark knew the rules and was aware his friend was breaking Ma's number one rule. He hoped his friend did not get caught. Brian told Mark he knew the risks and he was prepared to accept the consequences if he and Lacey got caught together.

He went searching for one of Lacey's friends who knew which house her parents lived in. He kept digging until he found her home address and now had a place where he could find her on Sunday afternoon and during the week. Brian decided about noon that Sunday to visit Lacey while she was at home. He wanted to be with her again, and this was the only way he could until next weekend.

Brian walked up onto Lacey's front porch and knocked on the door. Her father answered the door that Sunday afternoon. He asked her father if he might be able to talk to his daughter for a few minutes before he had to go back to Fort Benning. Lacey's parents gave Brian permission to speak with Lacey for a while.

He waited for her to come outside so he could talk to her without her parents and siblings being inches away. Brian knew what she did for a living, her parents did not, and she wanted to keep it that way. He looked at her standing there on the porch, no makeup and his chest ached. Brian had it bad. He wanted this young woman more like she was in her home than he had ever wanted her the nights they had been together at Ma Beachies.

"What are you doing here you know what will happen if we get caught together?"

"I know, but I do not care I want to be with you. I want to talk to you every second of every day. Lacey I cannot get enough of you."

Brian motioned for her to take a walk with him. She agreed and as they walked and talked about the weather and everything else, they could think of ways to keep from talking about the real problem at hand. They walked for a while until they came to Lacey's favorite place in the park where they could sit and talk. No one would bother them, and no one could sneak up on them and overhear what they were saying to each other. He hoped she could not tell what was happening to him while they sat there. This was so embarrassing for him. Brian had never wanted to be with a woman more than once or twice before, but he could not get enough of her.

He and Lacey sat there talking, nothing more. Brian found just being in her presence was enough for him that Sunday afternoon. She made him tingle all over, making him want her in ways he could not understand. Sometimes he wondered if what she did for a living was why he could not get this girl out of his mind, but he found the more time he spent with her the more her occupation did not matter to him. He was falling in love with her, not her body.

As Brian walked Lacey back to her house.

"I realize I am not supposed to ask you this, but I. cannot seem to help myself. Is there a way we can be with each other someplace other than Ma Beachies? I want to know everything about you, Lacey. I realize I am asking you to break the rules but there is something going on here that goes beyond what happened between us last night. I cannot get you out of my mind, I cannot sleep, I cannot do anything but think about the way you make my body shiver, and I get excited all over again."

Lacey just stood there and stared at him. She did not have any idea what to do or think. Lacey could not tell him that she was having the same type of feelings he was. She could not come up with an idea of what she was going to do, but she was aware of what she wanted to do.

He understood they would have to be careful doing what they wanted, but they did not care. They were falling in love with each other and wanted to be with each other more than once a week. Neither of them wanted their love to be dirty or an affair. Lacey agreed to go out with Brian on Sunday's from then on. She was aware she was breaking the rules, but she did not care. Her Sunday's belonged to her, and she could do with them as she pleased. Lacey did not think what she did on her own time was Ma's or anyone else's business. She had no idea Ma had asked the other employees in the house to monitor the movements of the weekend girls. They were having trouble with those who worked on the weekend falling in love with the men they spent their time with and quitting. Leaving Ma in a bad position without someone who could bring in the needed revenue working weekends.

"Brian, you must forget about me and what we share at Ma's. It would be in your best interest if you just put me out of your mind. But to tell you the truth I want more from you as well. I do not like the person I am there. I want to be me, again. With what I am asked to do there I dislike myself. I am a whore. Brian, I want my body and soul clean again."

Lacey looked up into his big brown eyes and at that moment realized he was staring at her. When their gaze met, it was like skyrockets exploding inside both of them. They wanted each other so badly they could hardly control themselves, but there was nowhere for them to go. Nowhere for them to take their relationship to the heights they wanted.

She would have to settle with being able to rub his hand with her delicate fingers, but just being near Brian was making the situation worse. Lacey felt as though her insides were going to explode, she was so attracted to this man. She had no clue why he of all people affected her this way. He was not her type; she had never met anyone who affected her in this manner this quickly.

Lacey and Brian walked the last couple yards back to her house. She kissed him on the cheek, goodnight as she stepped inside. Lacey realized she was taking a chance even seeing him. When she was inside the door, she leaned against it and let out a breath. She thought she had been holding her breath since she and Brian started their walk. Lacey knew June was nosey and loved to gossip. If she noticed Lacey with anyone, she would run and tell Ma Beachies what she had seen before realizing what Ma might do to her friend.

LACEY AND MA'S SWING TIME CLUB

Lacey came in on Friday night as they scheduled her to work ready to face whatever her job threw at her. She had made her clients as happy as she could. Lacey realized she could do nothing about her situation. She was going to make the most of her time at Ma's. Lacey came up with a way to remove herself from her work. She, more than anything, wanted to keep her home life separate and be the person there she wanted to be everywhere else, but she knew for a while she had to be two different people. It was the only way she could keep her sanity. Lacey was having a tough time with what she was doing for a living, all those ugly feelings she was having because of the lude things she was having to perform with her body just made her see herself that much worse.

Her first client of the evening was an older gentleman who claimed he lived out of town. He had heard about Ma's and Lacey from some of his friends. She looked at him with those big blue eyes and asked him what he wanted from their night together.

"Are you going to do any gambling tonight?" He told her he thought he would gamble a little if he felt up to it when they finished upstairs.

She asked him how much Ma had told him about what was going on at Ma's. He told her she had told him about the cost for an hour was one hundred dollars, but he saw no way he could last an hour with anybody. He would gamble if she did not exhaust him during their exploits upstairs. It would be then he would make his way back downstairs and into the gambling room which he had heard so much about.

Lacey did not realize he was a United States Marshal who officials gave the job of going in undercover to determine if he could get enough dirt dealing with the goings-on in this house. He had every intention of not allowing Lacey to get past first base. Sure, a Marshal was way above the means of any prostitute he had just met. His bosses had advised him to get Lacey to reveal details about what was going on at Ma's, but he found after a while he was having trouble keeping his mind on his job.

She started by taking her time with him. Kissing the corners of his mouth she knew she had a tough one here. Lacey had seen and heard the determination in his voice and the look on his face when he had spoken of Ma's prices for an hour with her.

She took the back of her hand and ran it across his cheeks. He could feel the softness of her hand and its warmth on his face. She lifted his hand kissing the ends of his fingers. Lacey began very softly to slide his finger in her mouth in a provocative motion to get his blood flowing. She did each of his fingers like this, he could feel each one of them relax and go limp when she finished with them.

Lacey took the pillows off the bed, arranging them on the floor in front of the fireplace. Come over here and have a seat beside me. She patted the floor beside her. Before he did, she took and unzipped the zipper on his blue jeans so she could reveal every part of his body. He slid his pants the rest of the way off and laid them over the foot of the bed. As he sat down beside her, she unbuttoned his shirt. She slid her arms around his waist and with one quick move she removed both his button-up shirt and his t-shirt, revealing the rest of himself to her. To be a few years older than she was he was not a bad-looking middle-aged man, so she thought.

She caressed his manly parts to his surprise he reacted to her. He sensed he could not resist Lacey's attention to him. As she was massaging him, she kissed his naval putting just a slight pressure on it. When she moved on up his body with her tongue, she found both his nipples to be hard and firm, little plums for the plucking. She kissed them both and one by one she wrapped her tongue around them and tugged just a little on them. Kissing them then nibbling on each she moved back down to his manly parts. With it hardened she slipped her tongue around it and then into her mouth. Afterward, she took her tongue and slid it up his abdomen, his chest up onto his neck. Nibbling on both ears he made a groaning sound she knew as the beginning of ecstasy. Lacey kissed the corner of his mouth causing him to open his mouth just enough with the motion she recognized the signals he was giving her as he wanted her to kiss him full on. She was not ready for that yet though she kissed the other corner of his mouth. Moving back down to his part she stimulated earlier; she climbed on top of him. She kissed the tip of his nose, the corners of his mouth again this time being tender slid her tongue into his mouth. Kissing him slowly and gently, taking in every part of his mouth. As he tasted her on his lips and in his mouth, he could not get enough of the blonde-haired girl. He wanted her more than words could say. Lacey knew he was hers for the taking but she wanted him to relive her for the rest of his life. He felt everything she was doing to him as well; she had a pleasant and inviting way about her. Feeling like he was floating he arched his back to move with her to get as much of her as he could. Lacey saw him surrender everything he had been holding back. She got up off him, took his hand and guided him to the floor where she had laid the pillows. She lay down, opened herself up to him. Lacey had sex with him. He kissed her on her soft nipples and her breast responded to him. Her entire body quivered with excitement as he was having his way with her. She wrapped her legs around him to get him closer to her. Kissing her she could feel his tongue inside her mouth. She could taste him, and she liked what she was feeling from him.

After a few minutes, they rolled over, and Lacey was back in charge. She was having her way with him; he wanted as much of her as he could get. She was kissing his chest and nipples when he rolled her over again. When he finished, he could not believe what had happened to him. She excited him and wanted her all over him. He never had a woman make him feel the way she had made him feel. He knew he was in trouble, he never wanted her to stop.

When finished, he sighed in disbelief somebody like her could have that kind of effect on him. He wanted more; he could still taste her kisses in and on his mouth. His body could still feel her touching and kissing him in ways he had never dreamed possible. When he finished, he sank down beside her! They lay there on the floor for a few minutes just staring into each other's eyes. He wanted more, but he knew he had to go. This encounter with Lacey had left him too spent to go into the gambling room. His brain could only think of her and what she had done to him in that hour. Nobody had ever made him feel like that.

He knew he had to pull himself together because he had to go into the gambling room next. Collecting evidence there would be easier than it had been with Lacey, but he had what he needed there and was now moving on. He felt something with Lacey he had never felt before, but he had a job to do and was intent on seeing his undercover assignment to its conclusion. As he left, he laid the hundred dollars on the night table. She knew he had realized she had done something to him no woman had ever done to him before. Looking around she was proud of herself that night.

In the back of her mind, she wondered why Brian had not come to see her yet tonight. For the previous two months he had been there as soon as he got liberty, but not tonight. She missed him so much, but she knew she had a job to do, and thoughts of Brian would have to wait.

Lacey had two more clients before midnight that night. The first was a first-year schoolteacher who needed some relief from the hectic week he had had at school. Teaching second graders was a much more taxing job than he had ever imagined. That night he needed some tender loving care, and some gambling afterward to take his mind off the world outside those walls.

She led him upstairs to her room. When she reached her room, she sat him on the floor where she had arranged the pillows for her next client. She asked him what he was looking for from his night. He could get out one word, he was in a state of ecstasy. All right then, you have to put your trust in me to give you what you are looking for.

Lacey found her job was easier if she just placed herself on autopilot and let what came to her flow. She began by unzipping his blue jeans, moving them down to his ankles. Untying his shoes, she pulled them off one by one. She now could slip his pants the rest of the way off leaving him exposed to her. Sitting there in the dim light of her room he could see what she was doing to him. Lacey unbuttoned his shirt exposing his t-shirt that was a brilliant blue.

As she kissed the corners of his mouth, wiping her finger across his cheek he could feel the warmth of her hands and fingers. It had been a long time since he had been with a woman. Lacey kissed his ears and the nape of his neck. She could see he was relaxing. All she needed now was for him to surrender to her, leaving him open to her to give him his wish of ecstasy.

Lacey wrapped her arms around his waist and slid her hands and arms under his. She lifted them and removed his blue T-shirt leaving his body open to hers. While he was not looking, she dropped her dress leaving her naked there in the room with him. She kissed his chest with her pouty lips. She ran her tongue along the line between the nipples on his chest. They hardened for her leaving her with the opening to pull on one until he let out a yelp. After that, she did the other one the same way, and with his eyes closed he let out another yelp. She knew he was not in pain; he was close to receiving what he had asked her for. A little more encouragement would be all he needed to fall off that cliff he wanted so much to experience.

She massaged his part which had been last to arouse. It had left her wondering a little if it would he get into the moment, but there it was showing some life. Lacey kissed him all over to arouse him. As she did, she took her tongue she slid it up his stomach to his chest into his Adam's apple. She kissed him on the corners of his mouth and slid her tongue into his half-open mouth. He wanted more of her he could smell her strawberry and cream scent filling the room. Intoxicated by her he wanted to fill all her tongue inside his mouth. He helped her search his mouth for every corner; he wanted more. Giving himself over to what was happening he returned her kisses. Wanting all her strawberry mouth as close to his as he could get it.

Lacey made him lie back; she put one leg on either side of his body. On top of him, she slid his manly part inside her. Moving up and down together one minute, one minute later letting her do all the work. While she was massaging him with her body on his, she felt him surrender to her. He moaned a sigh from deep within his soul. She knew he was hers to do as she pleased. Rolling him over she opened herself up to him and allowed him to follow the contours of her body. As he finished, he moaned again releasing of all the tension he had come into her room with that evening. Calm he was hers to do with as she pleased for the few seconds. She moved her body up and down on him to allow him to experience everything there was to offer. When he was exhausted, he sank into her arms where she held him for a few minutes.

Getting up and getting dressed, she asked him if he would gamble that night. He said he thought he would for a little while, but then he had to go. Lacey had made him feel, in a way, he had never felt before. After what had taken place with Lacey, he needed some rest. As he left, he placed Lacey's money on the nightstand in her room. When she had cleaned up and changed clothes, she went downstairs to see if he was still there. He was, but he was not doing so well when he saw her; he told her he thought he would go. His mind was still in Lacey's bedroom; he could still taste her and feel her on him. He had never had another woman make him feel that way.

Her last client that evening was a soldier from Fort Benning. Surprise overtook her with the soldiers' appearance. He looked to be even younger than she was. Lacey asked him what she could do for him. She really was not his type. His type would have been male standing about six-foot-five weighing about two hundred and ten pounds. He told her he had come there that night on a dare.

Lacey looked at him and asked him if he would prefer to gamble instead. He assured her he would. At least, he did not lose the bet. He came in; he tried to get into a woman, but he could not do it. She took him into the gambling room and that is where she left him. Lacey came back occasionally, to see if he were having any luck but he was not. He left broke, but he let Lacey believe he was having the time of his life. A few hours away from the base gave him the chance to charge his body how it needed, and to him that was enough.

Lacey already thought of herself as a slut doing the job, she had forced herself to take, to make a living. She wanted more out of her life. Lacey was looking for any way to make herself believe she could become a better person than the one she became in such a brief period. She wanted nothing more than to take control of her life again. She wondered where the girl who occupied her body just two months ago had gone. Lacey could not look at herself in the mirror without crying and wondering how she had gotten to this point in such an abbreviated period.

Lacey had seen Mark the weeks before. He did not have the same effect on her as Brian, but she liked him and could see herself seeing him as a regular. She took Mark upstairs to her room. He thought she was like the girls from the small town he was from. In the last two months, she had found two men she liked, a lot. Not just for the sex but for themselves most of all. Lacey could see having a future with either one of them if circumstances had been different.

Lacey did not feel as trashy when she was with Mark. He made her believe in herself and left her with the impression that she was special. Lacey needed some kind of distraction from the thoughts she was having about herself. She led him to her room where she sat him down in the chair in front of the fire. Lacey reached in and unzipped his fly, maneuvering his blue jeans to where she could see his skivvies. She could tell the touch of her hand, and her touch to his body already aroused him. Lacey massaged Mark's parts as she aroused him. As she massaged him, she kissed his nipples. When he let out a small yelp of excitement, she took his hand in hers and kissed his fingers one by one. After that, she stuck his index finger in her mouth and sucked on it. He let out another yelp of ecstasy. She could tell when the men were about to lose all control of themselves, she could then do whatever she wanted with a man after that during her night with them. He would be a willing participant in anything she suggested.

She slid herself down onto his awaiting parts that she had aroused. Lacey could tell he was hers for the taking. She felt him as he slid inside of her. Her body liked the warm parts of him inside of her and the way it made her body tingle. She moved her body up and down and sometimes even side to side with him. Lacey could tell he was over the moon at this point, yielding no point in turning back for either of them. Even if she wanted to, she could not stop herself or him now if she tried. She leaned down and kissed Mark on the nape of his neck. Leaned up and nibbled on his earlobes, all the while she is sliding her body up and down on his. She was aware of every inch of his body under hers. He looked up at her, with longing for her in his eyes. He wanted her to do whatever she wanted to him. It was such a good high to be in her arms and under her total control.

Lacey felt his hands on her back and the back of her arms. She wanted him to touch her, to get to know her. He moved up and down with her. He picked her up never missing a stroke inside of her. Mark carried Lacey to the bed where he laid her down. He climbed back on top of her. She felt him as he reentered her and moved ever so tenderly inside her. They were reacting to each other as one, moving back and forth with the rhythm of what was going on inside of her. Lacey wrapped her legs around Mark to get him as far inside her as she could get him. She wanted all he had. When they finished this time, they let out a yelp together which seemed to come from their hearts.

After their time together, Mark got dressed. On his way out he left the money on the bedside table. She walked with him downstairs to the gambling room. Lacey turned to him to let him know she would be back in two minutes. She went back up to her room to clean up and change her clothes.

About thirty minutes later Lacey came back downstairs and sat down beside him. He was having no luck with the cards; the feelings she had left him with distracted him. She was all he could think about. Lacey saw his expression and she could tell something was wrong.

"Mark is there a problem? "

"Yes, there is, but it will be okay I will get over it."

"Did I do something wrong?"

"No, it is my problem not yours."

After the next hand of cards, he got up and left. Mark Mitchell left Lacey sitting there at the card table not knowing if she had done or said something to upset him that night. So, she got up and walked back to her room to wait for the next customer of the evening. She did wonder if she would ever see him again or if he would ever speak to her after that night. Lacey had no clue what was wrong with Mark Mitchell, she was too consumed with her own problems to worry about anyone else's.

Ma and Andy

"Ladies, some of the other employees have brought some things to my attention that have been taking place after hours. Matters which involve some of you having issues with what we ask you to do here. We recommended, in the beginning, you remain free of any emotional entanglements because they can lead to jealous boyfriends. We cannot have that. We expect everybody to focus on what is going on here at the gambling house and upstairs."

"Everyone here is aware that gambling and what happens upstairs pays our bosses. We cannot have anything jeopardize that cash flow. Without the cash flow into the house, we would be in a world of trouble. Men not coming to the house would leave us with no way to pay our bills or our bosses. Our bosses are not men to mess with they are dangerous and have a lot of influence with people in places of authority here and outside of this area. Please remember there is always someone who watches you and me every minute of every day. If they find you doing something, I have warned you against, there will be consequences for you and to the person they see you with. So be careful and follow the rules we have laid out for you."

"Ma Beachies is a place where men of all ages come to relax, put their feet up, and find a little fun before going home to their wives, and their humdrum lives. We provide them with something to look forward to after a long day at the office. We present our soldiers across the river with something to look forward to when they take liberty on Friday night. Nobody could give anybody anything if they recognized each other.

If we learn you are having a relationship with someone you met here, there will be repercussions for you and the other individual. Do not get into that position and you will not have any issues growing out of what you do for us."

As Lacey turned around to head towards her room at the top of the stairs, she noticed her brother standing in the doorway to Ma's office. She knew he had been at home Sunday afternoon when Brian came by to see her. Lacey did not know if Andy had seen her leave with Brian or if it was someone else who was giving Ma her information. Lacey could not think about the goings on with Brian she was too shocked to see her baby brother in a place like Ma's. She had no idea, until that moment, that he was working for Ma Beachies Swing Time Club.

Lacey and her family thought Andy found work for some wealthy man in Columbus. When he came home on weekends, he always carried a wad of cash in his pocket. He made a point to not speak to his parents about his job and they respected his privacy and did not ask a lot of questions about his work. Lacey understood at that moment why Andy kept his occupation to himself and what kind of people he was working for.

June was beginning her position for Ma Beachies on a week that was extremely slow. She realized right away she liked the atmosphere. She could not find any reason not to do an unbelievable job for Ma. June's first week ended as one of those that was slow. This was what went on most weeknights, men thought the women worth having were there on Friday or Saturday night. It would take two or three weeks for men in the small town to hear about any new girl who started to work at the Swing Club which would be worth their time during the week.

Her first client was the District Attorney of Phenix City. She saw no significant issue with him, took him to her room where she could perform her magic on him. June sat him in the huge armchair in front of the fire.

As she was working his zipper down on his trousers, she teased him with her kisses. She unbuttoned his shirt, all the while, she is kissing his lips in a fashion that was teasing. He wanted her so much he could taste her. He found the aroma of her Sweet Pea perfume enticing and wished to get a better whiff of her. June kissed him very nonchalantly and provocatively. She slid her tongue far enough into his mouth to make him sigh with expectation.

When he played along with her, craving her even more, she took her palm and caressed the part of his body she was aroused by all of this special attention. June took her tongue and passed it up and down on his aroused part. She proceeded up to his body to his naval kissing him there in ways she figured no one had kissed him before; from the sigh, he let out. She returned to his aroused part and ran her mouth up and down it. He felt as though he was going to require something besides her to hold on to. When she made her way to the bottom of his body, she ran her tongue up his abdomen again. This time when she passed his belly button his nipples were hard like peanuts. She first put the left nipple in her mouth and very gently covered it with her tongue. She tugged at it; he cried out in ecstasy for he did not realize what she was doing to him, all he perceived was he liked the feelings she was waking in him. Next June proceeded to the right nipple, wrapped her tongue around it and gave a tug. When he cried out again, she was aware of the fire in her rise. She took her teeth and gently nibbled on the ends of his nipples. June knew the moment he gave himself to her.

He preferred her to make him feel good, and that is what he was getting from her. June was not one of the weekend girls he heard so much about, but she was making him feel every bit as enthusiastic as others told them of the feelings those special weekend girls gave them.

After a few minutes, she stood him up so she could slip his slacks off without a lot of effort. She took her hands and removed his underwear. June wanted nothing between her and him when she would have her way with him. She then took her hands and ran them under his shirt. As she lifted his arms, she pulled his unbutton shirt off and in one swift movement slid his shirt off his body. She realized he was acting he was under her spell. As she took his shirt off, she kissed him on the nape of his neck, sucking ever so lightly on his earlobe. He could do nothing about anything she was doing to him. She dominated him, prompting her to slide her tongue back into his gaping mouth. She kissed him very slowly, as he did all he could do was demand more. He could not seem to get his eyes to open so he was not aware of what she was going to do to him next. June took a cube of ice from the water glass resting on the bedside stand and ran it down his chest. As she did, she kissed where the water ran down him and left a trail on his skin. He was aware of her smooth lips and hands-on him and wished her to touch him all over his body.

June arched her back to climb on top of him. She sat down onto him and was aware when he slid into her. She moved up and down onto him. He made a sigh from the bottom of his throat. She held him enthralled for some time to come like this. June reached over to the bed and threw some pillows into the floor. She took her arms and hoisted her body off his. With her hand, she took his hand and led him to the floor where the pillows were lying waiting for them. June got him to sit down beside her with little effort at all. After that, she asked him to lie back onto the pillows and she slid him into her once again. She had him move up and down with her, experiencing every part of him inside of her. He could sense every part of her while he was inside as well.

He rolled her over moving up and down on top of her. When he finished, he sighed a huge groan of relief? She had discovered parts of his body that had affected no one or anything in years.

June made him tingle he could not think of anything except what this immature girl could do to him. He did not remember a time in all his years if he ever experienced another reaction like this. To him, wonderful was all he could express about her, she was the most exquisite woman he ever laid eyes on.

They had advised her when she finished with him; she was to take him to the gambling room, but he had no desire anymore to gamble. He could not think straight, he needed to get some air before he had to make his way home. June had worked her magic. When he left, he left her the cash he owed Ma plus a large tip for her.

With that one client she had made more than she had ever done in a regular job. She was hooked. June realized she had found something she was good at. Something she could call her own.

She had three more clients that night. June worked her magic on all; same as she had the DA. No one could claim she did not know how to give someone an enjoyable time. She made more that night than she had in a full month everywhere else.

Ma told June at the end of the night; she had done an outstanding job. If she kept it up, she would move to Friday and Saturday nights before she knew it. Why would she want to disappoint Ma? If I make my money during the week, why can't I stay during the week? June was right. She was bringing in business during the week and Ma saw that as a good thing. They would have to talk about her being the permanent weekday girl.

June worked the entire time that first week. Making such an impression on her clients she had problems containing herself.

She had been relaxing on her front porch when Brian came to Lacey's that Sunday afternoon. As soon as she saw him, she strolled inside the house so no one in the neighborhood would put two and two together than she had seen Brian and Lacey together while she sat on the porch. She had seen him visit Lacey at Ma's twice and she was aware of the rules. June spied on them from her living room window as they strolled down the street alone. She knew the rules at Ma's and as they walked down the road, she got the keys to her car and followed them. She sat in the bushes for a long time, watching her best friend and Brian break the one rule Ma Beachies warned them would have dire consequences.

June had promised Brian he would regret turning her down. She thought now she had found the perfect way to get even with him. June was not thinking about how badly she would hurt Lacey with the information she was supplying their employer. June was angry and there was nobody that was going to get away with what he had done to her.

LACEY AND MARK

He came in on Saturday night looking like he had just been through World War III. Mark sat down at the bar for a few minutes to have a drink before even thinking about what else he wanted. Ma's place always had whatever you wanted when you wanted it and this Friday night, he needed something, but he did not know what. Her establishment, over the years, gained a reputation as a place that took care of the soldiers and men from the town in a way none of the rest of them could match.

Mark told Ma when she walked up beside him, he would like to see Lacey after he finished his drink. She told Mark to give her a few minutes to ask if Lacey was free for a return customer. When she came back, she had Lacey in tow. Everyone was always glad to see Mark and the guys from Fort Benning. Their returning to the house every week was how they made their living. Without the working women in Phenix City, the soldiers would have nothing to do, except get into trouble in Columbus, Georgia. There were pros and cons to these houses being in Phenix City even for the commanders at Fort Benning.

After he finished his drink, he followed Lacey to her room. Asking her if they could talk for a while so he could get the last week of his life straight in his mind. He had survived survival training, which everyone said would be the roughest week of his life. Mark was still reeling from the last week and needed a friend. Lacey sat on the end of her bed while Mark shared his week with her.

Mark got up off the bed where he had been sitting. Walked over to Lacey and unbuttoned her dress. He took his hand and swept the dress from her body. He unzipped his blue jeans, unbuttoned his shirt, and took his shoes off, yielding himself vulnerable to her. Tonight, he was going to be in charge he was going to make love to her instead of the other way around.

He kissed her lips smelling the strawberries and cream he was always so crazy about. Mark slid his tongue into her mouth slowly. He wanted to explore and discover every inch of her mouth before the night was over. She found she wanted more of the man she was asked to take care of moments before and had been consoling about his week in the woods.

Mark backed Lacey against the wall beside the fireplace. They made love, this was the first time she had been the receiver and not the giver. Mark stood there giving her everything he wished to share with her. She felt safe in his arms and wanted more. He did not want her to move, but he wanted to be as close to her as he could. He picked her up without moving her he laid her on the bed continuing to make love to her the entire time. She gave herself to Mark that night. When they finished, she let out a sigh from the pit of her soul, she found with him what everybody else found with her.

When Mark finished, he sank down on top of her. They lay in her bed for a while talking. Exhausted after the week he had, and she was spent from the joy of having him. Mark got up to go downstairs to play some poker. He left her money on her bedside table for neither one of them wanted anyone to think she had developed feelings for anyone who came to Ma's for a little action.

Mark won a few hands of poker that night but lost it all back to the house when he made a few careless bets. He got up to leave; he already had plans of going to his sisters' house that weekend. Mark, tired from his time in the woods wanted to just kick his shoes off, but he could smell the strawberries and cream of Lacey on his body. He wondered when he would see her again after they finished the next two weeks; he had already gotten his orders to go to Korea to fight on the front lines. It broke his heart that his time with Lacey was nearing an end. Mark was aware he might not see Lacey again. Anything could happen to him while he was serving his country.

ALEX AND MARK

Alexander Benjamin Mitchell had called himself Ma's number one bouncer every day for the last two years. It was a surprise when he ran into his brother outside of one of the local grocery stores, one hot, summer Friday afternoon.

"Are you Mark Mitchell?"

"I am."

"You probably don't remember me, but I am your older brother, Alex."

"Not really."

"It is okay, you were young when I left home."

He was in Columbus to get a few groceries he was planning to fix supper for his latest girlfriend. As he and Mark stood outside the store, Mark told him about the family having a get together that weekend and their sister wanted all her siblings there.

Mark had been young when Alex left home. Alex almost did not recognize his younger brother. Alex was the one who called out to Mark and told him who he was. As Alex and Mark stood there and talked for a few minutes, Mark told him about the family gathering at Emmaline's on Sunday afternoon.

"Mark I will try to make it to Emmaline's early on Sunday afternoon."

As Alex walked away from Mark, he accepted his invitation. He was aware of nothing pressing Ma needed him to do on Sundays since her club was closed for the day. The time he got off on Sunday he used the time as his and he did what he wanted on his one day of rest.

Alex wrestled with the invitation, but he decided he did not have to work that day he would put his pride aside this once and go to his sisters for a nice family dinner. He realized all his siblings would not be there. Only two of them were aware where any of them settled down after they left home to go to college. Or so they had been led to believe.

Then there was his youngest sister, he heard from her occasionally, and knew she was still in prison for her part in the store owners murder, years before. It broke his heart what had happened to her but there was nothing he could do to help her. She had gotten herself into trouble with the rowdy crowd she hung around with. Someday, she would get out, but it was not looking good for her chances anytime soon.

As Mark sauntered into his sister's home, everybody wanted him to tell them about what he had completed in the last three months. He started telling them about the training he was undergoing at Fort Benning and how base officials were contemplating not allowing soldiers to come across the river any more to get any kind of entertainment. Soldiers were being taken advantage of by management holding their monies for them. When they were too drunk, they would keep the monies until they came back to get their money. With the fear that Ma and her men instilled in them none of the soldiers would contemplate going back for any money. Soldiers found they were happy with the way they left things because they got out of there with their lives.

When Alex walked into his sister's house, Emmaline almost passed out. She had not seen Alex since the day they had buried her parents. Emmaline did not know where Alex had been living or how he was getting by. She walked up to him, and they stood there and talked for a few minutes. When they finished, they hugged. Emmaline looked at Alex and told him,

"Make yourself at home. There is food in the kitchen, drinks in the refrigerator. Alex, I am glad you came today. I hope you make a habit of coming to spend time with your family."

Mark and Alex were happy it gave them the opportunity to share the afternoon. They had not seen each other in years. Except for the night, Alex ran into him coming out of the store in Columbus, Georgia. Alex was curious about why his brother had been in a place like Phenix City, but he never questioned his younger brother about what he was doing there.

Mark volunteered to tell Alex that he was seeing one of the young women that Ma had working for her at the house. I was seeing Lacey Burt. I have been seeing her since I have been back in Columbus and wish I could be with her more. But there are those rules that Ma has that if you see the girls inside the house, they do not allow you to date the girls outside of Ma's for any reason.

Alex, she has a way about her that draws a man to her and if you are not careful, she will never let you go. I want to see more of her, but her heart already belongs to someone else. He is aware of what she is doing for a living; he knows why she is doing it.

"Mark, is he aware of the rules?"

"He knows that Ma Beachies has rules for her girls."

"Who is it?"

"Brian Wilchair."

"Did he meet her at Ma's or outside of Ma's?"

"At Ma's, I did not get to go one weekend, and he met her then. I do not think he has been back except twice since he met her. They meet elsewhere on Sunday's now. I have been seeing signs of him falling in love with her."

"You think it has gotten that serious?"

"I do."

Mark did not go into any more detail with Alex and the two brothers left the story at that point. They went inside to get something to eat. Emmaline barbequed ribs, made coleslaw, potato salad, and bread which she spread out on the dinner table and the counters so all they had to do was walk by with their plates and get what they wanted. All the siblings had an enjoyable time that afternoon. Everyone wondered if anybody had heard anything about their sister since she graduated from college. No one would admit they did not know where she had moved to after she finished school. Afraid the other siblings would think they were terrible for letting her make a life for herself alone. She was by herself and as far as they knew she liked it that way.

Mark was unaware, he had just given his brother confirmation of June's report of Lacey and Brian's meetings on Sunday afternoons. If Mark had realized what he had done, he would not have been able to live with himself. No one in Alex's family had any idea where he worked or what he was doing for a living.

June Benning - Snitch

June Benning proved to be a real asset to Ma. She did not fear any kind of retaliation if she called Ma's giving management information concerning the other girl's activities after they left work. June believed Ma paid her good money and everyone should follow the rules. If her boss required her to follow them, then so did everyone else. June thought her bosses should show no one any favoritism plus Brian turned her down and she wanted to show him what he would get himself into for wanting someone like Lacey.

In the time, June had been working for Ma she met all kinds of men in the course of her job. There were so many of them that came in during the week that requested her over the other girls. June made a name for herself. But the name she made being a snitch for Ma with the other girls and people that had no association with Ma Beachies was not one she could be proud of. In the course of her job with Ma, she met many prominent men who wanted to give her whatever she wanted. They tempted June to take it, but something kept telling her what she had at Mas could be temporary. Do not burn your bridges at both ends, the people you are trying to hurt might be your lifeline one day.

City Solicitor, Arch Ferrell became one of those men who came in just to see June and be in her presence, with no one seeing him enter the club every week. It did not matter what happened in town. He must visit June for just an hour. She could make the trials of the day go away for a brief period. That was something he needed during this election time. Arch had also heard rumors that Governor Persons had already sent someone to Phenix City, and they gone back to Montgomery and reported what happened to them while he visited Ma's Swing Time Club.

He was afraid the State was about to raid the city, but he found himself in a position that left him with no way to find out when it was coming. According to the person inside the Governor's office they were trying to prove everything citizens of the city told them about the goings-on there. Even who it was that was feeding "The Machine" their information. They found none of the rumors to be true, yet everyone was anxious. The Machine's informant was pacing like he was on a bed of nails he was so sure one man they sent to Phenix City was going to break and report back who the mole was in the State House.

Arch had no idea what to do, did he tell Hoyt, Jimmie, and Ma or did he let them find out when the Marshals came to town and closed their businesses? He would decide in a few days, today he wanted to spend time with June. There he found he could forget for an hour his knowledge of business in the small Alabama town.

Mayor of Phenix City during this time was Homer Cobb. He was a powerful man in town he already had a hospital named for him, but he had a secret. Homer liked to see the young women at Ma's and the Bama Club. He did not make a big deal about it, but he had his favorites. June was the girl he liked to see during the week. She could make him feel like a man again, and then he could go home to his wife to manage the stress of day-to-day life.

Lacey was the girl he requested on weekends. He would come in twice a week just to get both the girls to make him feel better. Homer always kept his nose out of the business goings-on in Phenix City and with that, they did not think that he was a member of the Machine. That was a good thing for him, nobody guessed what he knew about the criminal activity in his town. They could not arrest him for being human and wanting someone to take care of him.

There were other prominent men in town who got involved with "The Machine." They wanted girls who could take care of their wants and keep what they saw to themselves. When the State sent agents in to gather evidence, they expected everyone to follow protocol and hide the dealings of these clubs.

Bama Club had the same rules as Ma Beachies Swing Time Club. No girl or dealer who worked for this club was to talk to or date anyone from these establishments. Officials were serious about these rules, they did not appreciate those who would disregard them. It was unknown so far how far they would go to enforce these rules. Nobody, though, wanted to be their example of the consequences of disobeying their orders.

J. Hoyt Shepard and James H. Mathews owned the Bama Club and had opened a business that made loaded dice. They distributed these dice to the gambling houses for them to use after midnight on weekends when the tables changed. No one knew this except these two men what their factory was turning out and no one wanted to know anything about the sinister activities of the town. It was a real situation of do not ask do not tell and it will just go away.

ALEX'S TRUE ALLEGIANCE

When Alex did make it into work on Monday, he felt as though he were carrying the weight of the world on his shoulders. He walked straight to Ma's office and closed the door behind him. As they sat there and chatted, he told Ma Beachies about the discussion he and his brother had over the weekend. Ma stared at Alex and in a surprised voice asked him how he and Mark Mitchell were acquainted with each other. He confided to her that Mark was his baby brother. He had not seen Mark in many years. When he left to go into the army Mark had been a young boy. Alex admitted to her that he had no idea that Mark even had any memory of him.

Being able to spend the afternoon with his brother thrilled Alex. With the way the day had progressed at his sister's, it troubled him to learn of the encounters that were taking place between Lacey and Brian. Ma assured him she would come up with a plan to take care of Brian before the end of the week. Ma's conversation with Alex confirmed her worst suspicions of what was going on between Brian and Lacey. She had already decided what to do but now she knew she had to do it soon to make an example of Brian Wilchair with the other men who came into the Swing Time Club.

Ma remembered Brian from that first night he came into the Swing Time Club. She also remembered explaining the rules to him before his and Lacey's first night together. Ma realized the two of them would try to say, they never heard the rules explained to them. She expected them to try to cover up what they did with each other after she got off.

Over the course of the week, Ma decided how she would have her men take care of the situation with Lacey and Brian. She called Alex into her office asking him if he would have any problems taking care of Brian. Alex reassured her that Brian was his brother's friend, not his. As Alex stepped out the door Ma told him to take care of the situation and to take whoever he chose with him to help him take care of her problem.

"Alex, I do not need to know anything about the details. The less I am aware of concerning what transpires the less I can swear to if anybody ever finds out what is about to happen in Phenix City."

Alex waited until Sunday night when no one would be around the house. That way no one might be in the house's rear and discover what was taking place in the Creek below. He knew what he had to do but Alex was not without feelings. Alex was experiencing a twinge of remorse for the man Ma had instructed him to kill. Alex knew who Brian was and what he meant to Mark, but it was part of his responsibilities to take care of Ma and her girls. This time though he was having a tough time separating his job from his family.

Ma and the rest of the staff at the house did not realize that someone had already been into the house. He had gone back to Montgomery, drafted his report, and turned it into the Governor and the Marshal's office. Ma's would be the first business visited on Monday by those who were to conduct the raid the State planned.

This time the agent had been promised immunity from any kind of prosecution. He was assured he had the full backing of the department and the Governor's office. His orders were to do whatever necessary to get the evidence needed to shut all these places down.

LACEY'S SECRET

Lacey called Ma that Friday with the news that set the bosses to wondering who Lacey was seeing to have her missing work,

"Ma I am not coming in tonight. I have been feeling bad all week."

"Lacey this is two weeks in a row. I need you here but if you are sick, I do not want you giving the paying customers whatever bug you have picked up."

Lacey was going to take the weekend off and try to get a little better before she had to go to work the next week. Lacey being off another weekend did not thrill Ma, but she knew it was for the best if Lacey stayed at home.

When the weekend regulars showed up for the weekend and found out Lacey was not there, they did not want to see any of the other women. They decided they would go gamble that night instead. Lacey was what they came for on Friday and Saturday nights and without her there these men did not want to forsake her. Ma found out that weekend Lacey was her draw for the weekend, and she would do anything to keep her for the clientele that she served.

Lacey stayed in bed all weekend and well into the next week. Her mom suggested she see a doctor on Monday. Her condition was not getting any better and that concerned her. Lacey agreed to make an appointment with a doctor to find out what was wrong with her. Lacey's mother picked up the phone and called the doctor to get Lacey an appointment so she could get some peace of mind. They got her an appointment with the family doctor for later that afternoon. For the family, he will work Lacey in as soon as possible. It had been a busy couple of days for the Doctor's office since the hay fever and cold season had arrived early that year and was making its rounds.

When she got up that afternoon, her mom drove her to the doctor's office. When they got there Lacey told his nurse that she could not keep anything down. They got her to an examination room right away because they did not want her to give everyone else what she might have.

As they were getting started, they took some blood to complete a pregnancy test. It would take about three days to get the results back and, in the meantime, the doctor would give her something for nausea.

Lacey returned home and fell back into bed. Her appointment with the Doctor had drained her and she wanted nothing to eat. Everything she encountered made her sick. It took a few apprehensive days, but on Friday afternoon right before his office was to close for the weekend, her doctor called. It was his responsibility to break the news to her that she was pregnant. Lacey dropped the phone and sat down on the floor and began to cry. She realized she was unmarried. Her parents would have a fit. Lacey did not know what to do, but she realized she did not want to end her pregnancy no matter who the father turned out to be. She was aware she had a job that meant anybody she had been intimate with could be the father of her unborn child.

When the Doctor told her when she had gotten pregnant, she realized who the baby belonged to. Brian and Lacey walked over to their favorite spot beside the waterfall and made love. It had been one of the happiest days she had spent in a long time.

Lacey realized now she faced a huge problem. She worked for a woman who advised everyone any fraternization between clients after hours would meet with severe repercussions. Lacey could keep things secret until she missed her period that month. After she missed her period Ma would have a doctor paid by Ma herself come to give her a pregnancy test, and when the Doctor discovered she was pregnant, there would be hell to pay. Lacey was aware who the baby belonged to because she called in sick ever since Brian proposed to her. Being with no one else in the time since the proposal she did not want to enter a marriage being a whore.

Lacey's parents told Ma about the nice young man who took their daughter out to lunch on Sunday afternoons. To them, it was time their daughter found someone to settle down with and start a family. It never occurred to any of her family that this could be a problem for Lacey. Nothing was wrong with a nice young man taking an interest in their daughter.

It did not take much for Ma to uncover Lacey's secret and told it would cause repercussions right away. When the facts of Lacey's pregnancy became known Ma was furious. She told everyone she would take care of the situation. Lacey thought she meant she was going to do away with her baby. Little did she know they were planning on how to do away with Brian. He had created this mess, and Ma was of the opinion Brian was the one to blame. Lacey was Ma's meal ticket, every man in town liked blonde and sultry.

She would be let go by Ma Beachies because she was of no use to the Swing Club pregnant. Lacey would then be unemployed and expecting a baby she had to support. She sat there for hours crying and feeling sorry for herself. Just feeling bad because she knew what was coming for her and Brian because of her and their child. Lacey could have never dreamed what Ma, Alex, and her own brother were planning for Brian Wilchair. If they followed her orders in the manner Ma expected them to, Brian would be made an example for everyone who worked for the Swing Time Club and every other club in town. No one would dare cross Ma again.

Brian and Lacey's Secret Meetings

Brian and Lacey had been meeting every Sunday for the last six weeks at the dam on the Chattahoochee River. To them the consequences of their actions were not as overwhelming as their love for each other. They would manage whatever came their way when or if it ever happened. Brian and Lacey wanted to be together, and they were not too concerned with the rules Ma had set down when they met that first night.

Brian would bring a picnic basket full of food and they would sit under a tree and listen to the water as it spilled into the lower branch of the river. Sundays were a lot slower and neither of them had anywhere to be until late in the afternoon. All they did was sit and enjoy each other and talk. Talk about nothing except their desires for the future and what they wanted for each other.

Around five every Sunday afternoon, Brian would walk Lacey to her car and watch as she drove away. She had to be home by six to have Sunday dinner with her family. Lacey kept up appearances for her brother, Andy's sake. She knew if he found out anything he would go back to Ma and tell her everything that was happening between them. He was loyal to Ma Beachies and there was nothing that could change his mind. Not even his sister could break the rules and get away with it. Lacey had agreed to Ma's rules and Andy was paid to enforce those rules no matter who the person was who might find a way to bend the rules to suit themselves.

June had just gotten home when Andy drove up in front of his parents' house. She asked him if she could talk to him for a few minutes before he went inside. He walked over to where she was sitting and sat down in the rocking chair in front of her.

"Andy, I followed Lacey today and saw what she has been doing for the last six weeks."

"What is that June?"

"She has been seeing one of the soldiers from Fort Benning."

"Did you recognize him as a customer of Ma?"

"Yes, Andy, I did."

"I don't want anyone to get hurt but Lacey was told the rules when she started working for Ma."

"I don't want anyone to get hurt either, Andy."

"Which one of her clients was it, June?"

"It was Brian Wilchair."

"Thank you for telling me, I will take care of this situation from here."

"You're welcome."

"See you later, I have to go eat dinner with the family now."

"See ya!"

As Andy walked into the house he kissed his mother hello, sat down with his father to talk about what had been going on for the week. Andy's family was a tight knit bunch. As Andy and his father sat there and talked Andy began to wonder how he was going to tell Ma what his little sister had been up to for the last several weeks. He did not want the responsibility of telling Ma, but he knew it was his job, and he took that very seriously.

Lacey walked into the living room and sat down beside her brother. He reached over and hugged his sister and assured her he would be there whenever she needed him. Lacey had no idea he was planning to follow her and see if what he had heard from June was true. After supper, Andy decided he was not going to tell Ma before he had proof of what was happening between Brian and Lacey. It was not fair to Lacey to take June's word for it. He was aware Brian had rejected June, and this could be her way of getting even with him for not wanting to be with her.

Andy knew if what he had heard was true it was up to him to inform Ma of what was going on outside the Club. He planned to follow Lacey Sunday morning and see if June had been telling the truth. Andy hoped with all his heart that June was lying just to see Brian get hurt and a little karma for rejecting her. It was the hardest week of his life. He started several times to ask his sister what if anything was going on between her and Brian, but he could not bring himself to ask the question. Pressures of what he had to do was bothering him so much, Andy had to leave his parents early Sunday morning.

When Lacey left the house, Andy had moved his car up the street and parked in one of the neighbors' driveways out of sight. As she drove away Andy left far enough behind her that she did not see him. Lacey went to the dam to keep her date with Brian. Andy was standing in the bushes and watched from a distance for hours. As he turned around to leave, he had tears in his eyes. It would be up to him to tell Ma what he had seen with his own eyes happening between his sister and Brian. As he walked back to his car Andy felt as though his heart was going to pop out of his chest. He wished so much that he did not have to do what he knew must be done.

It was hard for Andy to sit through supper that Sunday afternoon. He was still heartbroken knowing he had seen his sister breaking the rules that afternoon. He knew he had to go to work that Monday and tell Ma about the situation with his sister.

It was not fair to him or Lacey, but he knew he had to do it or face the same consequences she and Brian were facing.

As Andy arrived at work, he saw Alex going into Ma's office. He knew he had to tell his employer what he knew, but he was having problems with who it was he had to give Ma such news about. Andy walked into Ma's office and shut the door.

"Ma, I have something I think you should know."

"What's up?"

"Lacey is seeing Brian Wilchair outside of the Swing Time Club."

"Andy are you sure?"

"Yes, ma'am. I followed her yesterday and saw with my own eyes what is going on between them."

"You and Alex know what has to be done."

"Yes ma'am."

Alex walked over to Andy and tried to make him feel better. He was having problems with this situation himself. Brian was his brother's best friend and Alex did not know how he was going to be able to take care of this situation, himself. These two men had a job they had to do, but they knew they were going to hurt family when they did carry out this part of their jobs.

SECRETS HAVE CONSEQUENCES

Brian had not been to Ma's in months; he had come up with a way he could spend time with Lacey on Sunday afternoons. Brian was taking a huge risk, and he knew it, but he had to take it. He was in love with this girl, he wanted her to himself for more than an hour and she had already told him how working at Ma's made her feel. Brian did not want Lacey to feel as though what they had was dirty. He saw what they were feeling for each other as special and beautiful.

Brian walked over to Lacey's parents' house. When he knocked on the door her father answered the door. He invited Brian to come in for a few minutes while he found his daughter. Brian was more than glad to come into the house to wait for her, any chance to spend the afternoon with Lacey.

As she walked out of the kitchen and into the living room Brian asked her if she would spend the afternoon with him. She was happy to see him at the house, she got her sweater and walked out onto the porch with him. Brian took her hand and asked her if she would go for a drive with him, he had found the perfect spot for them to have a picnic, and no one would disturb them that afternoon. Lacey wanted time with him away from the ugliness of Ma Beachies, so she went with him.

Brian had found a spot by the 14th Street Dam where they could sit and be alone. No one could see them where they were. If anyone walked up on them, they could see and hear them before they got anywhere near where they were. He and Lacey sat and talked for hours. Brian told her he would leave in two weeks for Korea, but he wanted her to wait for him to return. He had gone by the local jewelry store on Saturday and picked out an engagement ring for her. Brian had asked Lacey to marry him a few weeks before, and she said, "Yes."

He took his hand and slid her over beside him. Brian kissed Lacey in a way they had never kissed before; slowly their tongues rushing to meet each other. She unbuttoned his shirt and blue jeans he took and slid her shirt off her body. He unbuttoned her pants and unzipped them. Brian let his pants fall to the ground. Lacey stood up, and hers fell to the ground as well. Sitting there in that secluded spot beside the Dam they made love to one another. It was slow, passionate. Done in a way that was tasteful and something she could hang onto until he returned. Their bodies moved as one when he raised his body, she rose to meet him. They discovered each other that afternoon in a way she had never known before. It was soft, something she had always dreamed of. When they finished, they sat there in each other's arms just looking at the water crashing over the dam. It was a beautiful afternoon; they wished never had to an end.

They got dressed, and he drove her home. She was happier that afternoon than she had been in a long time. Brian had asked her to marry him when he returned from Korea. He was the man of her dreams in every sense of the word.

Little did anyone suspect Ma had ordered a hit on Brian. He would get liberty for the weekend at any minute. Brian would be going to his parents' home to spend a nice night at home. One of Ma's men caught him before he got inside enticing him to go to Ma Beachies for a night of fun. Brian never saw Alex back in Pine Mountain, so he never knew that he was his best friend's brother. He was enticing him to follow him to what would be the last moments of his life.

Brian turned them down when out of nowhere the two men jumped him and dragged him to the creek behind Ma Beachies. Ma's men had stashed their weapons behind the club so when they got Brian where they wanted him, they would be in easy reach. Their weapon of choice was a baseball bat. One by one they took turns, one holding Brian and the other hitting him over and over with the bat.

He stumbled out of the creek bloody and battered. Brian could not walk let alone run from his assailants. Ma's men caught up with him and continued to strike him with the bat over and over. Brian lay on the side of Holland Creek for five hours before anyone saw him and called an ambulance. When help arrived, he had gotten such a beating that there was nothing anyone could do for him. Brian died at Cobb Hospital the next morning from internal injuries resulting from the beating he took with several baseball bats.

Someone shot Albert Patterson outside his car, beside his law office in downtown Phenix City that same night. They placed the butts of their guns against his face and pulled the trigger. Patterson tried to walk out of the alley where they shot him. He collapsed on the sidewalk in front of his law office. He was trying to get to the nightclub next door to try to find help. Patterson only made it a few hundred yards before he collapsed. There were two murders in Phenix City that night one everyone would remember forever. The other would not even make the local paper.

City Officials did not want to, but they were required to deal with the murders. Officials were required to call the State of Alabama to report the death of Albert Patterson. It was just a bonus for them to have to report the body they found in Holland Creek. None of them wanted to report Brian's death. He was a soldier from Fort Benning with what no one knew he had no one in the area that cared enough to come looking for him.

State officials were planning to come to Phenix City the next day. Instead of having to come to town for a raid they were now coming to investigate the death of two citizens of Phenix City. It was a bad way to get things started, but it forced the Marshal's office and the Governor to begin the investigation a few hours before they planned.

Instead of coming to town to investigate illegal business practices. State officials were now coming to town to investigate a prominent man's murder. After they found Brian beaten by the end of the day, he too was dead. The State of Alabama decided they wanted to make sure they wasted no opportunity. Nothing was too small for agents to investigate.

They planned to combine the death of Albert Patterson and Brian Wilchair into one case. With these murders, they gave Marshals enough to begin an investigation into everyone suspected of illegal activities in Phenix City. This was the break the Marshals had been waiting for. It was a shame two men met their death before someone would try to stop these brutal killings.

Now they could find someone willing to talk to them about what was going on in the small central Alabama town. State representatives tried for years to get someone to supply the information. Someone with firsthand knowledge of the operations would be a real help. Little did "The Machine" know their officer collected enough information to shut them down when he was in town and visited these houses and gambling businesses. He was a part of enough and had spoken to enough staff to build a solid case.

National Guard troops were in Phenix City 6 weeks before they were allowed to do anything. Governor Persons made a trip to Washington D.C. to speak with Dwight Eisenhower, and Herbert Hoover. They advised him to declare Martial Rule, it gave him more leeway than martial law. It was upon his return that he gave the order and declared martial rule in Phenix City. After a couple of days, General Hanna received the okay to begin closing all the gambling and prostitution in Phenix City. It was not long after that order that they began dragging illegal gambling tables, slot machines, ticket making devices out of the Clubs. By night fall they had a stack of illegal devices stored beside the county jail and was burning what they could not get to the jail impound yard. To the business owners in Phenix City it was a sad day, but to the residents and the Russell Betterment Association it was the day they had been waiting for. It might have taken a while, but they were getting what they asked the governor to do over two years before.

SAD NEWS DELIVERED

Mark stopped by Ma Beachies looking for Lacey when Ma told him, she no longer employed Lacey. He asked them if they had any idea how he could find her. Ma's day manager gave him Lacey's home address. He wanted to see her and find out why she no longer worked for Ma Beachies Swing Time Club. Mark and Brian were leaving in a few days, and he wanted to see her one last time before he left for Korea.

He pulled his car into Lacey's yard where Lacey greeted him with a huge grin. Mark wanted to see her one last time to be able to say goodbye. As they sat and chatted, on her family's front porch, the local sheriff drove up looking for Mark.

"Are you Mark Mitchell? "

"I am. "

"I just came from the hospital where I heard your friend Brian Wilchair was taken. Someone beat him to death with a baseball bat. Mark, I am so sorry to be the one to give you the sad news about your good friend."

"Do you know who could do such a thing to him?"

"Yes, we do. Mark that part of this is not going to be easy either."

"Why is that?"

"It was the bouncers from Ma's. I understand your brother is the one in charge and gave the order."

"What?" Mark replied.

"You did not know he worked for Ma?"

"I knew he worked for her, but I never dreamed he could do something like this."

As the two men stood there talking Mark turned around and stared at Lacey. How would he tell her about Brian? As the Sheriff drove away, he walked back to the porch and sat down beside her. Mark gave her the sad news about Brian and Lacey fell apart, sitting there in front of him.

Sobbing so hard her entire body shook, Lacey took a while to get out the words she must say to him. "Mark there is something I must confess to you about myself."

He was curious to learn what was so urgent now. Lacey stared at him; she told him she was pregnant. That the father was Brian; she found herself alone, with no one to help her take care of her baby. Mark, Brian came by the house two weeks ago and asked me to marry him.

"I said yes but I suppose that doesn't matter now."

Mark knew Brian was dating Lacey and would have been with her other than at Ma's. Lacey did not have any idea Brian was his best friend. He was going to take care of his friends' fiancé and his baby. In his mind, he saw what he was considering to be what friends did for each other. He sat down beside her and explained to her Brian, and he grew up together. Brian was his best friend, and he would do whatever he had to for him.

He stared at Lacey for a few minutes.

"Lacey you and I may not share the same kind of emotions you experienced with Brian, but it would honor me if you would let me take care of you and Brian's baby."

The idea overjoyed Lacey: she wanted her baby to have a father and a mom that cared for each other. And she did already have feelings for Mark. Mark waited for her answer; Lacey agreed to be his bride and to let him raise his best friends' child. It took a lot for him to control himself.

Lacey and Mark sat and talked for two hours that afternoon. Mark sat on her front porch, in the swing, telling her what he was told about Brian's death. Lacey could not find out that Mark's brother or even hers had been the ones to kill the love of her life.

Mark sat telling Lacey about the years he and Brian had spent in Pine Mountain and the Army. He got up walking around telling Lacey how the two of them had met. Mark needed someone to sit and listen to. He missed his friend and needed someone to talk with while he struggled to come to terms with the circumstances he knew, so far, about his murder.

As she sat in the swing, and he paced back-and-forth Mark told her that there had been four or five guys from Ma's who had taken baseball bats with them. Lured Brian toward Ma's and as they approached what looked to be a closed club, the two men walked by those who lay in wait and all of them jumped him. They tied Brian up to take him to the bottom of the cliff as the bouncers began to beat Brian in the head, the legs, arms, and some of them even aimed at his midsection. No one could figure out how he had endured the initial beating. How he clung to life with such horrific injuries long enough to inform authorities who the guilty men were.

Mark found out Alex had been the one to lead the men who beat Brian. He also knew that the other guys were Ma's bouncers.

As they sat there Lacey cried, uncontrollably. Neither of them could tell the other one that their brothers worked for Ma. They were in disbelief that anybody would kill Brian. Neither of them could think of anything he could have done, except be with her, to cause such a beating and his body left under a bush to die, alone, beside the river.

BRIAN'S FUNERAL

After the coroner informed Brian's family of his death. His mother and father made all the arrangements for their oldest child's burial. They would bury Brian in the family cemetery. Lacey went with Mark to the Wilchairs home the night they had the wake for Brian, but no one would have anything to do with her.

Mark attended the funeral and Brian's family received him with open arms, but they treated Lacey as though she was not there. No one in Brian's family wanted anything to do with her. She mentioned to his parents she was pregnant with Brian's baby, but they wanted even less to do with the baby. She stayed in the back of the room, alone, until Mark was ready to leave and strolled out of the Wilchairs home with her head held high. Lacey knew she had done nothing wrong and had paid her last respects to the love of her life. She would now go home and mourn his death alone.

Before she and Mark could get to their car Ms. Wilchair came out to speak with Lacey before she left to make the trip home.

"Lacey, we do not mean to appear stuck up, but we would rather not have any reminders of what happened to Brian. He was our child, and we would rather remember him as he was. His baby would be too big a reminder for us of what happened to him."

"I think I understand, but if you ever change your mind, you will know where to find Brian's child if you want to accept him into your family."

"Thank you, Lacey, but we prefer to just forget about the child. It will be easier on us."

As they strolled to Mark's car, he turned around and asked her what Brian's' mother had said to her. She told him what she had said. Mark was aware of how Brian's parents could be, but they never let him see this side of their character. He never dreamed they would reject a baby. This was something they had prepared no one for, and Mark intended to give Brian's baby the best life he could.

Brian was gone, but he had left behind an heir and a grandchild. This should have been the happiest thing to come out of this catastrophe. They, though, had made the entire situation ugly. Lacey hoped Brian's child never realized how his grandparents felt about him. She would watch after his child the best she could, but her heart broke every time she remembered Brian's parents' reaction to the child and to her. She swore to herself no one would ever hurt her child like that.

As Mark and Lacey got into the car, Mr. Wilchair approached her. He stared at her with his big blue eyes. She could see where Brian had gotten his good looks.

"Lacey, we do not wish to hurt you or the baby, but we think it would be better if you found someone else to raise your baby."

"Do you want me to put the baby up for adoption?"

"No, but you do not have to disclose to other people the baby is an heir of the Wilchairs."

"I will think about what you are proposing. I cannot agree that our baby will never have any idea who his father was."

"That is up to you, but it will get nothing from me."

"That is your choice." Lacey turned around, got into the car, and slammed the door and locked it.

"What was that all about, Lacey?" Mark asked.

"He wanted to tell me himself that they want nothing to do with Brian's child and will not tell anyone that Brian left an heir. He also does not want me to tell anyone, including the baby, who his father was."

"I am sorry. I never saw either of them act this way towards anyone."

"Mark, it is not your fault. Brian told me how they were when he asked me to marry him. Brian prepared me for this. I knew it was a possibility when I came to the funeral today."

"Are you okay with this?"

"Yes, I am. I had Brian's love for ever no matter how short of a time it was. Nobody can take that away from me, and they sure cannot have our child. It is their choice to miss their grandchild's life. One day they will change their minds."

LACEY'S DILEMMA

Mark wasE sorry to have been a party to the way Brian's family treated Lacey. He had never heard them talk to anybody like they did Lacey. Every time he visited their home his parents were nice to him. What he saw at Brian's funeral was a side of his family Mark had never experienced before.

As Mark and Lacey drove home, he asked her what she wanted from her life for the next 50 years. She thought for a few minutes.

"I want to show everyone I can provide for myself and for my child. I want to give my unborn child a stable home, with love and respect. I want something from a husband that I never saw in my parent's home. Sure, they love me, but I do not think they can stand each other. They stay with each other for us children."

"Mark, I do not know how I will support me and my baby."

"Lacey, we will figure it out."

"You say that now, but I am pregnant by Brian and when my parents find out, they will have a fit."

"Brian was my best friend. It would be my honor if you would allow me to raise his child as my own."

"Mark, what are you trying to say to me?"

"Will you marry me and allow me to raise Brian's child as my own?"

"I do not know what to say."

"Say Yes."

Lacey sat there, in silence, the rest of the drive home. She got out of the car in front of her parents' home. She turned to Mark and presented him with her decision about the question he had asked her.

"Yes, Mark, I will marry you."

"You will."

"Yes, I will allow you to help me and protect your friend's child."

"Lacey, you just made me the happiest man alive."

With those words, Lacey smiled the biggest smile Mark thought he could ever see on anyone's face. The only obstacle they faced now was how to get married before they shipped him off to South Korea. He was due to get on a military plane in two weeks. They were required to marry before that day.

It took a lot of effort; Lacey pulled it off though. She and Mark were married two days before he was to ship out. Mark found Lacey and their unborn child a home to call their own until he could come back to them. They prepared the babies' room in the brief time they had before he was to leave. She was ready to take care of herself and her baby after giving birth to him.

It proved to be a difficult delivery and Brian Anthony Mitchell came into this world by c-section while Mark was in Seoul, South Korea. He flourished and became a healthy, well-adjusted child by the time Mark retired and returned home.

Mark found a position in Columbus with the local police department. He was going to remain at home, with his family, from that day forward. Mark kept the secret that it was his brother who led the attack on Brian. He did not want Lacey hurt anymore by that horrible time than she had already been. Lacey was happy and beginning to blossom as a woman. He never wanted her or their child to experience any of the ugliness that went along with that time.

ARRESTS WERE MADE

"Ma Beachies Arrested" was one headline that shocked the citizens of Phenix City when they woke that Tuesday morning. The Governor of the State of Alabama had sent investigators to town to not only find the illegal activities inside the businesses, but now he was over the moon to have a full-grown murder to tie to the illegal activities. Officials found it satisfying to be shutting down the houses of ill repute. Nobody, however, knew what to think of how the papers reported that Albert Patterson lost his life. It was like a scene out of a movie they were seeing.

At Ma Beachies Swing Time Club when they arrested her, they also arrested June and some of the other girls who reported to work that Tuesday morning. No one warned anyone about what was coming because no one was told before the Marshal's arrived and padlocked the doors.

Lacey lucked out when she quit Mas before the raids happened. Marshals visited her home to see if she would talk about what went on inside the house on any given night, except Sunday. Lacey was more than happy to tell what she knew about the goings-on inside Ma Beachies Swing Time Club.

One of the men from the Marshal's office asked her if she was aware that her brother was one of the men who had beaten Brian to death. She told him she had been told that by her parents and she did not have any hard feelings towards him. Lacey thought she could never call him her brother again; him being one of the men who took the love of her life and her child's father away from them was more than she could forgive of anyone.

As Lacey talked to the Marshal's some of Ma's bouncers dumped the slot machines into Holland Creek. It was easy enough for them to do. All anyone had to do was open one trapdoor in the house and push the machines into the water below. No one ever found out but two of those same bouncers were in on having the secret switch installed on one table that would dump anyone who got out of hand out of the house and into the creek. Ma had covered all her bases, or so she thought.

They arrested Alexander Mitchell and seven other bouncers for Brian's murder and their part in other illegal activities. They were all sent to Birmingham and would stand trial there. All of them received life sentences and would never get out of prison. Even if they did, they had no job, or family to return to. Alex and Andy could never go back to their families and ask for forgiveness because they had taken the one thing both families loved the most in the world, Brian Wilchair.

CLEAN UP OF PHENIX CITY, ALABAMA

When the sun came up over the Chattahoochee River, the next morning, U.S. Marshals, and National Guardsmen began the huge task Montgomery sent them to town to carry out. Officials ordered them to arrest city officials named in warrants. When their duty concluded with the men who were in places of authority, then it would be their job to start with the people named in the warrants for illegal gaming and sales of illicit activities. No one had told them these were the people, the governor's office had tried for years to collect enough evidence against to put them in jail. For a long time, no one could tie them to any kind of crime. When the evidence came, it was like a laundry list of charges. They would arrest many highly respected people for their involvement in gambling, prostitution, and bootlegging and most of them would go to jail for many years. When Marshals raided most of the bigger night spots, they found the owners from other night clubs hiding among the customers. When national guardsmen finished arresting those, they knew to be running the clubs, it would be their job to arrest the men who in positions to protect the citizens of the small Central Alabama town and county. Individuals who citizens trusted as law enforcement officials to make sure the town was working in a law-abiding manner would find themselves in jail for their part. Residents did not know what was going to happen after the National Guard gave their town back to them, but it was a good start. As the marshals and guardsmen finished rounding up everyone named in the warrants that first day, they were ready to find somewhere to get some rest. If it was for only a little while before they had to start over. With the warrants of the owners and city officials out of the way. Next, they could focus on the employees. National guard could see, at least, three days' worth of searching and arresting people before they were anywhere near finished cleaning up Phenix City. They warned the employees of the arrests and many of them were fleeing to escape prosecution for their parts in the illicit activities. Everyone was concerned because this tragedy touched as far as they could tell every family in town. It did not matter where you lived, someone you knew, or a family member played a part in this cleanup.

Their activities of the past would leave their families to suffer the embarrassment for their husbands and father's involvement in the way Phenix City was making its living. For many years everyone had sworn that they were running a legal and respectable business in town, but when the National Guard was finished, the facts showed a totally different way of life. No one, for a long time, would know what it took to make a respectable living in the area. They would have to cross the bridge to find work for years to come. Those involved with gambling, prostitution, and bootlegging would carry the stigma of any association with the town. Given what they had done or ordered done they slept at night, like babies, even with the horrific knowledge of two men's untimely deaths carried out by people who worked for the Dixie Mafia. No one could imagine how long marshal rule would stay in effect in town, but they hoped it was not too long. Everyone needed to get back to work.

County Solicitor–Arch Ferrell was from Seale, Alabama. He was born into a well-established family of lawyers. Ferrell served as a captain in the army during World War II. Upon his return to Russell County, he was appointed circuit solicitor by Governor

Jim Folsom. Everyone knew Ferrell as a brilliant lawyer. They also knew him to have a problem with drinking and a sharp temper.

In 1953, he broke the jaw of one of his close friends, Jimmie Putnam. A woman in the RBA Auxiliary said that Ferrell would call her at home and threaten her without identifying himself. She proved she knew him by recognizing his voice when he spoke to her on the phone.

Ferrell bragged about his involvement in the Phenix City rackets claiming that he oversaw it all. With his position as solicitor, he had the power to prosecute or excuse anyone he wanted. Ferrell would advise Shepherd, Matthews, and the other gamblers on many matters.

During the May election of 1954, Si Garrett, attorney general for the State of Alabama officially backed Lee Porter. He had the intention of using Porter to keep himself in political power. Albert Patterson, running on the platform "a man against crime," beat Porter in the primary election. Garrett and Arch Ferrell changed the numbers on a recapitulation sheet to add votes for Porter. Garrett convinced county democratic party chair Lamar Reid that Patterson was the gamblers' candidate. Reid provided access to the sheets, with Garrett reassuring him later that "this voting thing comes up all the time."

When a Birmingham reporter found a discrepancy in the vote totals, he reported it in his paper. The governor's office called Garrett before the Jefferson County grand jury to testify on June 18. Reid had confessed, naming Garrett and Ferrell in his testimony as the men he had given the recapitulation sheets. After an all-day session in front of the grand jury, Garrett returned to the Redmont Hotel. During dinner Garrett had several calls between Ferrell's Phenix City office and Garrett's hotel room. All the calls were made while Garrett was enjoying dinner. He would later try to use these calls as an alibi for the Patterson murder that same evening. Si Garrett received a call a second time to testify before the grand jury. This time they questioned him about his involvement in voter fraud and Patterson's murder. After ten and a half hours of testifying, Garrett left Alabama and checked himself into a Texas mental hospital. In August, Garrett suffered a broken neck in an auto accident. He survived but checked himself back into the mental hospital. They never brought Garret to trial for either voter fraud or the murder of Albert Patterson. Hugh Bentley said, "It will probably take something bad happening before anything can or will change the environment in our town." He did not realize at the time how true his statement would be. It did not matter how big or small you were "The Machine" ruled Phenix City.

Governor Persons realized he was out of time when the news of Albert Patterson's murder, in the parking lot beside his law office, reached him. Ferrell pretended to find the identity of the men who had committed the murder. He collaborated closely with Chief Deputy Sheriff Albert Fuller to find those who had pulled the trigger killing Albert Patterson. After several weeks of no reported leads, the acting attorney general Bernard Sykes removed Ferrell from the murder investigation. After Ferrell's removal as lead investigator clues to the identities of those involved showed their true selves to the national guard who the governor had stationed in town. Their orders had come down that they would be there until they restored order in the small town. Attorney General Sykes realized Ferrell was protecting the men who killed Patterson, or even himself, and Albert Fuller. When the new investigators began to get those in town to talk, it surprised them to hear those men's stories. One who was with Fuller that night reported that he was there when Fuller placed the butt of his gun against Patterson's cheek and pulled the trigger. Another man, who did not want his identity made known, said he was with Ferrell when the order went out to kill Albert Patterson. Ferrell did not care how they got the job done, but he wanted it done that night. In his law office or out front, he wanted it where everyone could see who was in charge.

Solicitor Ferrell, Chief Deputy Sheriff Albert Fuller and Attorney General Si Garrett were all indicted for the murder of Albert Patterson. All three men would stand trial for the murder of Patterson but only one would ever see the inside of a prison for the murder. Everyone in town knew Ferrell and Garrett had used Fuller to carry out the murder of Albert Patterson so they would have someone they could lay the blame on if anyone ever went to trial. Fuller believed them when they told him they would take care of him; he never thought his friends could use him to get their dirty work done. Ferrell and Garrett let him take the blame for the murder and hoped their planning paid off.

Chief Deputy Sheriff–Albert Fuller had been raised in Phenix City, Alabama where he gained the reputation of being a bully. After graduating from high school, Fuller joined the Navy where he had been stationed in Texas. Which is where he learned to shoot and where he crafted his tough image. He thought wearing a white Stetson and cowboy boots made him look tough. When he returned to Phenix City after WWII he found a job with the sheriff's department. Albert Fuller gained power and influence in Russell County, creating his own position as Chief Deputy Sheriff. Sheriff Mathews allowed Fuller free rein over the county. Fuller partnered with Cliff Entrekin to run Cliff's Fish Camp, the most lucrative house of prostitution in the county. The prostitution business in Phenix City thrived under Fuller's protection, which anyone could buy for one-third of the income. Fuller recruited new prostitutes by arresting young girls looking for work in Phenix City nightclubs. The prostitution house operators would then visit the girl in jail and offer her bond for her working for them in their Clubs.

U. S. Marshal's arrested Fuller for the murder of Albert Patterson as he was recovering from a back injury. Fuller claimed the injury resulted from falling off a horse. Some believe his injuries more likely resulted from a feud between Fuller and Phenix City Night Police Chief Buddy Jowers over territory. Mafia bosses sent Fuller to find Jowers to collect protection money for his services, but he refused to pay. Some believe there was a scuffle and Fuller hurt his back in the altercation. That is one theory, there are more.

On March 11, 1955, they convicted Fuller for the murder of Albert Patterson. He served time in prison, released from jail, and later died with a broken neck suffered from falling off a ladder.

John Hoyt Shepherd was born in Alabama on August 22, 1899. His parents had moved early in Hoyt's life to LaGrange, Georgia where he was raised. Hoyt and his parents moved back to Phenix City during the Depression. Shepherd met up with Phenix City local Godwin Davis and learned the more lucrative craft of gambling. Jimmie Matthews, another new arrival, and Shepherd soon formed the S&M Syndicate, which supplied gambling equipment, including slot machines, roulette wheels, loaded dice and marked cards to local businesses. They also formed the lottery known as "The Bug." In 1938 "the bug" was so popular that patrons pushed into the Ritz Café, owned by Shepherd and Matthews, to buy tickets and see the winning numbers. The crowd exceeded the building's ability, pushing out the walls and a steel beam, collapsing the building on the crowd. Twenty-four people killed and dozens more injured. Police swore to be acting in this case but could turn up no witnesses to what had happened at the Ritz Café.

In 1952, as Phenix City was feeling the heat of community activists like Hugh Bentley, Shepherd, and Matthews announced they were getting out of the rackets. With their retirement they turned over a warehouse full of gambling machines. Though retired from running gambling clubs, they rented their properties to other gamblers. Later both served 90-day sentences for leasing buildings used for the purpose of gambling. A wiretap proved Shepherd as the leader in the Phenix City crime syndicate. Shepherd invested his money from gambling in legitimate businesses. He made donations to churches and financed political campaigns. Shepherd's goal was to change his reputation to one of doing good in his community. He later said he did it all for the sake of his children.

FINAL THOUGHTS
EPILOGUE

The beginning of the end of the bad old days came 65 years ago in June. Bosses murdered a Phenix City lawyer and reformer, and Albert Patterson's death led to the cleanup that followed. The National Guard moved in, and the racketeers moved on to other parts of the country. In the four months following the cleanup, a grand jury handed down 741 indictments. With a second grand jury issuing a final report an assertion that Phenix City was no longer "a modern-day Sodom and Gomorrah" like it had been for all those years before 1954.

Phenix City is still trying to get over that period in its history. They demolished all the businesses that were here in 1954, and Ma's has long since seen the wrecking ball to make room for the future. Family members still live and work in the area. Phenix City is a town trying to overcome its bad-boy history, but there are still officials in power who still believe they are above the law. Nobody is willing to go against the system in the small southern town today if it works do not fix it.

A week after the death of Brian Wilchair, Ma Beachies was raided, again. This time they did not have time to clean up their operations. Information from someone in Montgomery had given them the tip they needed naming the Sheriff, Police Chief, Mayor, and District Attorney as being on Ma's and Hoyt Shepherd's payroll. With this bit of information, they were led to what they needed to begin the clean-up process in Phenix City. But they did have evidence that no one could repute. Their deputy had spent the night with Lacey and had been shown the gambling room afterward it was really all they needed to shut down Mas for good.

Two days later, Albert Patterson was gunned down while he got into his car by those in town who stood to lose when they shut crime down in Phenix City. They had chosen Patterson Attorney General and were looking to him to clean up the town he called home. He was also a member of the Russell Betterment Society. They declared Martial Rule in Phenix City for a while until they could clean up some more unsavory areas of town.

Brian was killed because he broke the rules. He fell in love with a girl they warned him on many occasions not to try to see outside of Ma Beachies. Brian loved life and the thrill of risk-taking. They killed him for taking one of those risks, but a beautiful baby boy came out of that risk. A child he knew nothing about and that was a shame.

They shipped Mark out to Korea the next week. He returned to Phenix City two years later. During the time he had been away Lacey wrote to him every day. Telling him how the baby inside her was growing. After he was born, she sent him pictures of the son she had given him and Brian. In a letter home, Mark had requested Lacey name her baby Brian for his father and Marks friend. She was more than happy to do what Mark asked of her. It made her feel good to know Mark wanted their child to bear the name of their friend. Mark felt a pang of jealousy that he had not given her such a wonderful prize, but he was happy to raise his best friends' child for him. He knew if the situation were reversed Brian would have done the same for him.

Mark never told Lacey about their brothers being the ones who killed Brian that June night. He never wanted the ugliness of that evening to touch her again. Mark had been there when Brian's parents rejected her and Brian's child. He wanted nothing more for her than to take care of her and give her and her baby whatever they needed. Mark Mitchell would be the father Brian never got the chance to be.

They could hardly believe how lucky they were. They were raising Brian's baby together, making him happy and healthy. One afternoon, Mark walked with them to where the whole thing had started. Ma's Club did not fare very well, they tore the old house she had used down and no trace of it remains. An auto repair shop stands today where Mas stood the night, they killed Brian and Albert Patterson.

Ma Beachie was arrested for gambling and prostitution. She was never charged with the murder of Brian Wilchair. Ma was released and lived out the rest of her life in Phenix City, Alabama running the family store.

THE END